Deirdre Madden is from Toomebridge, Co. Antrim. Her novels include *The Birds of the Innocent Wood*, *Nothing is Black*, *One by One in the Darkness*, which was shortlisted for the Orange Prize, *Authenticity* and *Molly Fox's Birthday* which was also shortlisted for the Orange Prize. Her most recent novel is *Time Present and Time Past*. She teaches at Trinity College Dublin and is a member of the Irish Arts Academy, Aosdána.

NOTHING IS BLACK

Deirdre Madden

faber and faber

First published in Great Britain in 1994
by Faber and Faber Limited
Bloomsbury House, 74–77 Great Russell Street,
London WC1B 3DA
This paperback edition first published in 2013

Photoset in Palatino by Wilmaset Ltd, Wirral
Printed and bound by CPI Group (UK) Ltd, Croydon, CR0 4YY

Deirdre Madden is herby identified as author of this work
in accordance with Section 77 of the Copyright,
Designs and Patents Act 1988

A CIP record for this book is
available from the British Library

ISBN 978–0–571–29879–2

*The author wishes to thank Hawthorden Castle
and The Author's Foundation for their assistance.*

2 4 6 8 10 9 7 5 3 1

for Harry with love

BROWN: colour of *mole*, of the leaf that goes. Earth.

YELLOW: madness, sickness, fear. Part of the sun and of joy.

COBALT BLUE: electricity and purity. Love.

BLACK: nothing is black, really *nothing*.

FRIDA KAHLO

SHE ARRIVED in the town late on Monday evening. Kevin had phoned Claire that morning to say that she was on her way; he had seen her off some twenty minutes earlier. Claire had promised to collect the visitor. 'Be sure to be there on time,' Kevin said. 'She'll panic if you're not there.'

But Claire knew that the bus would be late: it always was. She had plenty of time to buy the things she needed: a chicken, a fruit cake, some real coffee; things which, while they could in no way be considered luxurious or exotic were not available in Rita's shop, and so could only be bought on her trips to town.

She put the things in the boot of her car, but didn't bother to lock up. The vehicle parked next to hers was a camper van with German plates and two mountain bikes fixed securely to the back of it. She walked down to the harbour. A damp stink of whiskey, smoke and stale porter wafted out from the swinging door of the pub as she walked past. It was almost a relief, masking, if only for a moment, the fishy stink that perpetually hung over the town. It came from the fish-processing plant. She'll notice that as soon as she gets off the bus, Claire thought. She had watched visitors arrive before now, seen the look of disgust on their faces as soon as they got a whiff of the air. But the smell wasn't as much of a problem as it might have been elsewhere, she thought, for the little town was so drab that there wasn't much from which to detract: a Londis supermarket; a chipper; a few pubs; a merchant chandlers, its window full of ropes and yellow oilskins: these, and a few other undistinguished establishments scattered along a straggling main street, with the houses painted in ice cream colours . . . yes, she thought, the fishy smell gave the place whatever character it had.

She took a packet of cigarettes and a box of matches from her pocket and lit up as she walked out along the pier, occasionally glancing back over her shoulder to see if the bus had arrived. Every so often she would stop and stand looking down into the few fishing boats moored there, taking in the texture of the thick, bright paint, the rough wooden duckboards on the decks, the plastic fishboxes. The trawlers were tied up to large iron rings which were pegged into the pier. She liked those rings, and always took note of them. She liked how the ring had cut its way into the stone over the years, for both metal and stone were hard, but the end result looked soft. Such greyness! The stone pier, the sky, the sea itself; only the cabins and hulls of the trawlers were bright, and the blue plastic fishboxes. It started to rain, that fine, penetrating, persistent rain that seems to come out of the air rather than to fall from the sky. It was the height of summer. She ground what was left of her cigarette under her heel. Glancing back, she saw the green bus draw to a halt.

In the huddle of tired passengers, she picked Nuala

out immediately, even though it was years since they had last seen each other. Claire couldn't help smiling when she saw how Nuala was dressed, and had to hang back for a moment, trying to keep a straight face before going up to her. Nuala was wearing a dark-green oiled thornproof jacket. Evidently she had dressed for the country, and had thought that this was what everyone in Donegal would be wearing. Claire also was able to guess which items belonged to Nuala out of the pile of luggage the driver was unloading from the side of the bus. The co-ordinated tapestry cases stood out from the rest, from the battered holdalls and the Gola sports bags. Claire was a bit alarmed to see how much she had brought with her, even if she was staying until the autumn.

It took about half an hour to drive to where Claire lived. She could see the relief on Nuala's face when she told her this. 'It's quite different out there,' Claire told her. 'Lots of fresh air.'

They drove out along the coast road. Claire would have admitted that the place where she had chosen to live was bleak, but she thought that it had its own magnificence too. It certainly didn't have the lushness and prettiness people often expected to find in the countryside. To appreciate this area properly required a certain way of seeing things. Because of the wind coming in off the Atlantic, it was never static. Claire liked that about it, and she liked the colours, not bright, but often vivid, with the contrasts of the low, soft plants against stone. The road ran high along the coast, over-looking headlands and small pale beaches. After a certain point it veered right and ran through a stretch of bogland, past cut stacked turf. The grass was grey there, not green, grey against the rich dark brown of the cut earth. The grass looked dry, the peat was a moist brown . . .

Suddenly she remembered Nuala, who was sitting silently beside her. 'Not too much further now,' Claire said. Nuala nodded, but said nothing. After the bogland the land rose again, there was a scattering of coloured houses, and then they saw the sea again. There was a vibrant blue building with a name above the door and an ad for Guinness in the window; further on a little shop; on again and there was a white cottage, set back from the road. Shortly after that, the road simply ended, and near this point there was a small, grey, stone house. It stood on a headland, and the land rose steeply behind it. A short, hedgeless lane linked the house to the point where the road ran out. A narrow path continued on down to a cove sunk deep in the headland.

Claire lived in the grey stone house.

When people came to stay with her, it made her more alert to things than she might usually have been, so that she found herself looking at them as if it were also her first time there. What she noticed in town was the smell of the fish. What she noticed here, as soon as she got out of the car, was the air itself, the sharp freshness of the wind off the sea, mixing with the sweetish smell of peat smoke.

Throughout the journey Nuala had said very little, responding to the comments Claire had addressed to her, but asking no questions and voicing no opinions of her own. Claire wasn't sure what was going on in her mind: was she shy, anxious, sulking? She had had a long journey, Claire remembered, she was probably tired.

4

She helped Nuala carry her luggage into the house, and showed her to her room. That was always a difficult moment. Some people would be clearly disappointed, or even shocked, by the austerity of the room in which they were to stay. But Claire didn't mind this. What she found much worse were the people who gushed delight. She knew that they hated it far more than the people who made no attempt to hide their chagrin. Some visitors pretended to be ecstatic about the idea of staying in a stone house in the far west: waking in a room with a painted wooden ceiling and bare sanded floorboards, sleeping in a high, narrow iron bed, having no furniture but a wardrobe, a dressing table and a kitchen chair. With some people, even as Claire opened the door and showed them the room she could see that they were mentally calculating how long it would be before they could decently make their excuses and flee the spartan conditions.

Some people pretended to themselves as much as to Claire that they liked it, and for a week or two they did enjoy playing at the simple life: baking because it was the only way to get fresh bread; buying fish locally and gutting and cooking it; carrying in turf for the fire. The novelty would last, on average, about a week and a half. Claire always knew that the end was approaching when visitors started to talk about food a lot, particularly about their favourite restaurants. Soon after that, they would leave. Some of her guests, those to whom she was closest, would ask her frankly what possessed her to live in such a hole.

Nuala didn't react at all when she saw the room. She simply nodded, and put her cases down beside the wardrobe.

'The bathroom's next door. Come downstairs when you're ready, I'll make some tea.' Claire was moving away when Nuala said, 'Can I see your studio first? I mean, can I see it now?'

Claire was surprised. She nodded, and led Nuala along the landing, pushed open a door. Nuala stepped inside and looked around. North light fell on the white walls, the stacked canvases, the old shoeboxes with labels describing their contents gummed to the lids, the squashed metal paint tubes. Everything was extremely neat and tidy. Nuala looked all around, and nodded. She walked over to the window, which overlooked the headland and the sunken cove. Out in the bay there was a small island, little more than an outcrop of rock, with a lighthouse on it. The sky was immense. Claire held the door wide, indicating that she wanted her out. 'I'll see you downstairs,' she repeated.

Claire had finished her tea and was smoking her second cigarette when Nuala appeared. They sat together for a while. Claire felt ill at ease. 'Do you want to ring Kevin?' she asked, but Nuala said, 'No. He's to phone me this evening.'

Eventually Claire said, 'I'm going out now.' She stood up and put her cigarettes in her pocket. 'I want to go for a walk. It'll rain later.'

'How do you know?' asked Nuala.

Claire smiled. 'It always rains later,' she said.

2

AS SHE PUT ON HER ANORAK, Claire wondered which direction she would take today. She decided to walk up behind the house to the cliffs, for she felt constrained, and wanted the height above the sea rather than the restricted arc of the bay. She walked for about half an hour, until she was on a narrow sheep track, beyond which was a sheer deep drop to the sea. The ground was uneven, and she sat down in a curved depression which gave some semblance of shelter. The noise of the sea and the wind calmed her.

For some reason, Markus came into her mind. It was a long time since last she thought of him, and she didn't know why she should suddenly find herself remembering him now, much less that particular day when they had sat together in a café in Germany, and he told her about his visit to Poland. Where was it he had been, Cracow or Łódź? She couldn't remember now. He had been affiliated to an art college for six months and he had told her that when they showed him the accommodation provided it turned out to be in a building which had been a Nazi headquarters during the war. People had been tortured and killed there. Someone told him the interrogation rooms had been in the basement, in the part of the building which had since been converted into showers for the students. On the façade of the building there was a marble plaque, a memorial to those whom the Nazis had killed there.

'I took one look round the place,' Markus said, 'and I just knew that I could never live there. I couldn't bring myself to live in a place where things like that had happened.' He had found lodgings in an apartment in the city centre.

And did it matter so much,' Claire asked, 'what had happened there?'

'Yes, of course,' Markus said. 'It mattered to me.' He said that he could not live in a place where there had been such evil. 'And you seem to be forgetting what nationality I am,' he added coldly.

She remembered feeling embarrassed at that; feeling ill at ease too, talking of such things in the comfort of the café. It didn't seem right to her. It had been Markus's idea to go there. He took a childish delight in such places: the white coffee pots and the rich cream cakes, the dark wood of the bentwood chairs, the newspapers attached to bamboo frames: 'It's all so civilized,' he would say, which annoyed Claire.

He could relax in such places, he was more open with her and would tell her honestly how he felt about things, such as how he hadn't been able to bear the Halls of Residence. He said that sometimes he felt redundant as an artist, and that it was hard to be vilified, but harder still to be ignored. 'People in Europe now aren't interested in art because it has to do with death. It teaches you how to die, and people don't want to know about that. In that way art is religious. There was always, until this century, a distinction between things which were true art, connected with religion, and things which had a social function, which were decorative or for entertainment. Now we have only two divisions: money and entertainment. What matters is making money, and then you rest from that by being entertained with what people like to think of as art.'

The irony was that Markus was a successful artist, and at the time they met in the café, he had been commissioned to make a sculpture for a bank. He was confused by this: pleased but troubled. He told Claire he knew that when he was younger he wouldn't have accepted such a commission. He said he still didn't understand why they had asked him. On the one hand, he was appalled to find himself in the pay of such philistines. On the other he was relieved to have the money. 'I'm not such a fool', he said, 'to think that people who go to the bank will see this work and suddenly they will appreciate it. I don't believe in taking art to the people. If they want it, they will find it. If there are people who go to the bank who already have some appreciation of art, they may like the work I do, but those who are not interested will not be converted.' He looked sad and wistful as he talked to her about this. He knew all about artistic integrity, and he felt that he was selling out. He reminded her of an adulterer who spoke sadly of how wonderful a woman his wife was, and how she did not deserve to be betrayed even as he continued to deceive her.

The waitress had come over then, and he had brightened up, taking out his wallet to pay for the coffee and cakes. Claire couldn't imagine Markus without money:

not that he ever had a great deal, but he would never have less than enough, would never allow himself to slip into the precarious financial predicaments she often found herself in. The waitress, who was wearing a frilly apron, rummaged for change in the expanding leather wallet attached to her belt.

Claire had once visited a concentration camp. When she was in Munich, she had visited Dachau. She didn't want to talk to Markus about it. It had been a strange experience to be there, not at all as she had expected. It left her feeling empty.

She had realized then how evil can affect a place, leaving not the sense of horror one might expect, but instead killing off all its spiritual energy and leaving it sterile. Dachau was a museum, spotlessly clean. There was a laundered prison uniform in a glass case, and she had watched a tourist take a photograph of it, against the light, with a simple camera. Claire knew that it wouldn't come out properly. At best he would get a black, headless outline against a bright background. The meticulous care with which the exhibition was presented unsettled her. She found it more telling than the museum itself, and thought it wrong that it was the people who had perpetrated this terrible thing who now were explaining it. It was a false expiation. She had once seen a photographic exhibition of Dachau, as it now was, and the exhibition consisted of photographs of the signs dotted around the place: 'This way', 'Turn right', 'No entry', which the visitors were to follow obediently.

Markus put his change in his pocket. 'How would you feel about living in a house where someone had killed themselves?' she asked. He looked at her blankly. He had obviously lost the train of the conversation. 'Would you be able to live in a house like that?'

'Of course,' he said, realizing what she meant. 'That wouldn't be a problem, because there's a difference between evil and suffering. I cannot tolerate a place where evil has been done, I tell you, I could not live in such a place. In whatever house people have lived, there will have been suffering, and happiness too, and if someone has gone so far as to kill themselves, then there has been extreme suffering. That I can accept, for I feel pity, not horror. To live freely and at peace in such a place is to show solidarity with the suffering of the past.'

Years had passed since that day which she now remembered, huddled on the clifftop. There were so few places left that were not steeped in blood, which you could say with certainty had not been the scene of some atrocity in the past. She liked this spot because she felt that it was not saturated with human experience in this way. She wondered where Markus was now, and what he was doing. It was years since she had seen or heard from him, and she regretted having lost contact with him. She had loved Markus.

The ground where she sat was turfy and springy. She leaned over a little tussock and examined it carefully, teasing out with her fingers the tiny plants of which it was composed, the mosses and the lichens. The combination of smallness and complexity in the plants fascinated her. She put her head right down on the tussock as though it were a pillow, and closed her eyes, listened to the sea, the birds, the wind. She never regretted having come to live here. She opened her eyes and saw, inches from her face, a tiny spider scale a blade of grass. Where was Markus now? She sat up and looked out over the ocean. Claire thought of the woman she had left back in the house, and hoped the period of time they were to spend together would go well. She wondered what Nuala was doing. Would she still be drinking tea? She imagined her sitting by the kitchen table, her hands around the teapot for warmth, looking out of the window at the headland which would be vividly green against the sky's soft grey. Would she notice that? Claire knew already what she would find when she returned: the obscurity, as if a room could be flooded with darkness, just as it could be flooded with light. The dim warmth of her house suddenly seemed enormously desirable to her. Coming back here had been the right thing for her to do. She stood up and started to walk back.

3

AFTER DINNER THAT EVENING, they sat by the fire. Nuala leafed through some of Claire's art books, while Claire pretended to read. She found it impossible to concentrate, and kept looking over the top of the book she held, to scrutinize her visitor.

It was less than a week now since her father had rung. She'd known at once that something was up, but could never have guessed what he was about to say to her.

'Nuala wants to come and stay with you.'

'Who?'

'Nuala,' he said. 'You know, your cousin. Auntie Kate's daughter.'

'That's who I thought you meant. She's the only Nuala I know. Or rather, don't know.' Claire was mystified as to why her cousin would want to come and stay with her. 'How long was she thinking of spending here?'

'A couple of months,' he replied.

'Daddy, is this some kind of a joke?'

'I wish it was,' he sighed.

As he started to explain, the door behind Claire creaked open. She turned around and stared from the hallway where she stood back into the sitting room she had just left. A painting hanging there caught her eye. It was a small canvas: a still life in oils of a draped cloth, some fruit, and a brass jug. It was an austere work, the objects imbued with the moral rigour of Alice, who had painted them; Alice, who had been prodigiously gifted; Alice, who had been in Claire's class at art college, and who died within two years of having graduated. Claire continued to look at the painting as she talked to her father.

'What exactly is the problem?' she asked.

'Well, it's hard to know for sure. Kevin says she needs a rest, she's very tired.'

'Are you saying she's depressed?'

'No, not exactly. Kevin says there's more to it than that.'

'Oh great,' Claire said. 'Just what I need for the summer.'

'Ah now, Claire, don't be like that.' And by the pleading tone in her father's voice, she knew he wanted her to say yes. 'Family's family, after all. She took it very hard when your Auntie Kate died. And don't worry, it isn't that she's depressed. I asked Kevin particularly about that, because I thought if she was, maybe it wouldn't be such a good idea for her to go to such a quiet place.'

'What do the doctors think?'

'They think she ought to get away from the city, get away from everything for a while.'

Claire didn't respond. She was still staring at the painting. 'Hello? Are you still there, Claire?'

'Yes I am. Listen, Daddy, it's all right. She can come here if that's what she wants.'

'Ah, aren't you very good.' She could hear the relief in his voice.

'Yes, I am, aren't I?' she said.

'By the by, you're not to worry about money. She'll give you a good amount for her keep each week. Kevin told me to be sure and tell you that you wouldn't be out of pocket.'

He would say that, Claire thought, but she made no comment to her father.

'I think Nuala would like to get away as soon as possible: certainly within the week, if that's all right with you.'

Claire said that would be fine. They chatted about a few more things and when she had finished she put the phone down, went back into the sitting room and wondered aloud to herself in the empty house what she had let herself in for.

Nuala's late mother, whom Claire still spoke of as 'Auntie Kate', had been a sister of Claire's father. She had left Donegal as soon as she finished school, moved to Dublin, got married, changed her accent, and tried to convince everyone, not least herself, that she had never lived as she dismissively put it 'up the country'. Nuala, who was her only child, was exactly the same age as Claire, and the two cousins had nothing in common. There had never been any hostility between the two branches of the family. Instead, a kind of uneasy affection prevailed, and they silently and amicably agreed to differ. 'We've always given each other the benefit of the doubt,' Claire's father had said, after a rather stilted visit when Claire was a teenager. She'd never forgotten that remark.

Nuala and Claire had never had much occasion to be together, as they lived so far from each other when they were children. True, Claire had gone to art college in Dublin, but Nuala was at university by that stage, studying economics, and they moved in completely different worlds. By a strange coincidence, Kevin had been in Claire's year at art school: he'd been one of her best friends at that time. Nuala and Kevin got married within a year of their leaving college. Claire's parents went to the wedding, and over the coming years they kept her posted with news of the couple which they heard through Auntie Kate and Nuala's father, Uncle Jack. When Nuala and Kevin bought the restaurant, when they moved house, when Kevin had a minor car accident, when Nuala became pregnant: by means of her parent's weekly letters all this news found its way to Claire, wherever she was, first when she was travelling on the Continent, and in more recent years when she had moved back to Donegal. She wished them well, and followed their lives with detached interest. The last thing she would ever have expected was that Nuala would express a desire to come and stay with her. And yet there she was now, sitting in the chair opposite Claire and leafing through a book about the mosaics of Ravenna with a desultory air. Claire realized with a start that this woman was in many ways a stranger to her.

Suddenly, Nuala looked up and caught Claire watching her. She didn't comment on it, but only said, 'You've been there, haven't you?'

'To Ravenna? Yes,' said Claire, 'I have. Of course, a book like that can only give you an idea of what it's like. Reproductions never do full justice to works of art, and it's particularly the case with mosaics.'

'Why is that?'

'Well, the colours aren't accurate, for one thing. You can't get the effect of light and space in a photograph like that either, and the mosaics are integral to the architecture of the churches. The scale, the light, the texture, even the atmosphere: it's all so different when you're actually there.'

'You really think so?' said Nuala. 'Funny, I always enjoy looking at pictures in books much more. You can see the details better there. Sometimes in churches the paintings are so high up you can hardly see them properly at all. And art galleries are generally far too crowded, you can't get close enough to the paintings to have a proper look. I remember going to see the *Mona Lisa* in Paris, and I just couldn't believe that this was what people were making such a fuss about: just this dark, ugly painting, so far away behind a pane of glass. After that I thought, well, I'll never believe anything people tell me again. You can tell the biggest lie and people will believe it. I bet out of every hundred people who go to see the *Mona Lisa* ninety-nine of them are disappointed, but they're too unsure of themselves to admit it.'

'But you should always remember when you go to a gallery,' Claire said, 'that the paintings you see there were never meant to be displayed or viewed in such a way. I doubt if Ravenna would disappoint you.'

But Ravenna had disappointed Claire on her first arrival there, for the town itself was not as she had expected it to be. Ravenna, Corinth, Carthage, Rome: she had realized afterwards that cities with such names could never adequately fulfil the expectations one had of them. And so it had been with Ravenna. Never before had she seen a place from which history had so evidently and dramatically withdrawn. Only when she went to the churches did she find what she had looked for, found more than she had expected. Nothing could have prepared her for the impact made by that strange combination of dimness and vibrant colour, the coolness of the buildings and the vivid, shimmering images they contained. The frieze of women on a gold field: she remembered the sense of motion conveyed by their pointing feet, each figure different, each an individual with her shawl and almond eyes. She remembered the looped curtains of the Emperor's Palace, the curved boats on a sea of tessellated glass . . .

It was a long time now since she had visited Ravenna, but her memory of it was still strong. She realized there how her beliefs had changed, without her even having noticed it: faith had withdrawn, just as the sea had abandoned the city. And yet it was in Ravenna that she had begun to appreciate for the first time the spiritual dimension of art. The arrogance of it, for Theodora and Justinian to have their portraits put up like that in a church, above the high altar beside representations of Christ and the saints. For all that, the images of the dead faces touched her more than she could understand. Is this the only possible immortality? Nothing more than this? The decadence of it, the richness of the gold, and the shimmering colours. The Imperial portraits were a strange combination of vulnerability and brute power. She remembered going outside afterwards into the curious lightness of the air, and how frail and lovely the world had looked. For days afterwards she could not stop thinking about the mosaics, was haunted by them, not wanting to believe how much of existence was embodied in those stern faces.

She realized that Nuala was looking at her expectantly, and somewhat ironically. She was glad when, just at that moment, the phone rang. It was Kevin, calling for Nuala. Claire discreetly closed the sitting-room door. When Nuala came back into the room a short while later, she looked abstracted and had evidently forgotten about the mosaics.

The next morning, immediately after breakfast, Claire went straight to her studio. Even before Nuala had left Dublin, Claire had sent a message to her making clear that she would be busy working every day. In autumn she was to have an exhibition in Dublin, and because she had so much to do before then, she was anxious to establish early that she had regular patterns for work which could not be interrupted for visitors.

She sat down and made a quick watercolour of the view from her studio window, which looked out over the headland. This was an exercise which she performed first thing every morning when she went to the studio, as a sort of warm up for the real work of the day. When her work went badly, she would have the consolation of having accomplished at least that. She had been doing this exercise for quite some time now, and this morning, when she had finished, she looked back at some of the earlier landscapes. The view from the window never bored her. It was different every day, and she liked the act of concentration it required to look at it every morning and paint it as though she were seeing it for the first time ever. Not just how things looked, but what one could actually see was dependent on the weather. It was extraordinary how the colours could vary from one day to the next, now vivid, now murky. Sometimes the red and white lighthouse would be obscured by the heavy rains and mist that came in off the Atlantic, sometimes it dominated the picture, bright against the grey sky and the sea. As she looked back over the earlier paintings, she wondered for how long she should continue this practice. She also wondered why these exercises should be so satisfying, because they remained just that, exercises. Although she often struggled with her real work, and was dissatisfied with it, she knew that to try to devote herself seriously to landscape painting would be a serious mistake.

Elsewhere in the house, Nuala was settling in. Having unpacked everything she had brought with her, she realized that her possessions looked absurdly grand in the austere room: the green oiled jacket hanging from a nail behind the door, her diamond rings and pearls on the dressing table, her folding leather alarm clock on the chair beside the bed. She had been annoyed to learn that she couldn't lock her room: Claire said that the key had been lost. She went to the door and listened carefully. She could hear Claire moving about in her studio. She left the door slightly ajar so that she would be able to hear if there was any movement down the corridor. Then she opened one of her cases and took out a silk handkerchief which was wound around a small, rigid object. Sitting on the edge of the bed, she unwrapped this thing.

It was a teaspoon: a silver teaspoon with the crest of the Shelbourne Hotel on it. It had all started with this, she reflected. God, if Kevin knew she still had this . . . !

Well, he didn't know. What was it her mother had always said, 'Well, I'm sure if Daddy never finds out, he won't mind in the least.'

Of all the things she had . . . acquired (that was the word she had carefully selected to refer to these objects) over the months, this was the only one which really mattered to her. It was the first and only thing she had really wanted, and it was still redolent of the strange emotions of the whole business.

How long ago was it now? Six months? Yes, about that. It had been a day in January, a wet day. She always hated January. She'd bought herself a new leather handbag that afternoon, but she was unhappy when she came out of the shop, so she had gone to the Shelbourne for coffee and cakes, choosing to go there precisely because she knew she would pay over the odds. Somehow that was important. The handbag had been outrageously expensive too. She didn't understand the logic behind these things. Were they supposed to make you feel good simply because they cost a lot? Maybe it was the fact of being able to have them that was meant to be satisfying, rather than the object itself, she thought as she sat in the hotel. She realized that she was coming to the end of a brief binge of compulsive spending which worried her while she was involved in it in a way the other business would not. It had started in November, just after her baby daughter was born. She didn't think it could be connected to that, though, because all the things she bought were for herself.

She would bring home the items she purchased and show them to Kevin, sometimes even telling him that they'd been more expensive than they actually were.

She wanted him to understand that there was something wrong; she was asking him to help her. But she was so confused herself that she didn't know how to ask, except by pulling some dress or jacket from its bag and saying, 'What do you think of this? It cost me a mint.' But Kevin never understood. He would only ever say, 'It looks great. Really suits you. Don't worry about the money. You work hard, you deserve to have whatever you want. The restaurant would never have been a success if it hadn't been for you.'

The purchases were experiments as much as anything else. No matter how much the shop assistants would coo at her about it being a dress that would take you into the evening or the suit being easy to wear, she would know even before she bought it that it would make no difference. There'd always been a faint hope, though, hadn't there? Every time she went into the changing room there was always the idea that when she stepped out and looked in the mirror, she would see someone else looking back at her, her old self would have vanished.

But when that failed to happen, it still wasn't enough. She always had to see the thing through to the bitter end. The experiment was never over until she had watched them run the slide over her credit card, signed on the dotted line and received the ostentatious bag with the name of the shop printed on it. Experiments. Bloody expensive experiments too, but that day had been different. Something had happened.

She'd been looking at her reflection in a huge mirror, and the sales assistant had been wittering on as usual, something about how it was a bag you could use in any season, when suddenly Nuala interrupted her.

'I'm going to die,' she said.

The woman stopped talking and stared at her. Nuala realized the misunderstanding at once and was about to add 'So are you', but she thought better of it. The look of pity and confusion on the other woman's face was more than she could bear. Nuala held the handbag out to her.

'I'll take it,' she said coldly. The assistant completed the sale with minimal conversation. As she handed the bag over, Nuala could see that the other woman was on the point of tears.

She left the shop and went straight to the hotel, ordered coffee and sandwiches and cakes, and decided that she would damn well get a taxi home too, just to finish things off. She hated shopping on her own, that was the truth of it. She'd always gone into town with her mother every Friday for the whole day, and only now did she appreciate just how much she'd loved that. It had made her feel powerful to be out with her mother and be able to buy the best. There'd been something conspiratorial about it too: assessing lampshades or choosing shoes or trying out lipsticks on the backs of their hands, there was a closeness that was beyond words.

The waitress brought her coffee, and as Nuala stirred it, she noticed the spoon, noticed how heavy and cool it was. She put it on the saucer, and continued to look at it as she drank. And then something quite extraordinary happened.

She realized that she wanted the spoon. No matter that the name of the hotel was stamped upon it; no matter that she had at home a splendid canteen of silver cutlery, a wedding present she had never used; no matter that she had access to any amount of spoons and forks in the restaurant. No, it was that spoon and no other she wanted, and she had never wanted anything so much since she had been a child. How she had longed for things then! She remembered longing for Christmas, longing to be six, to be grown up, above all to have particular things, which were filled with magic by the very fact of her wanting them. The hotel lounge was practically deserted. It would be so easy . . .

The bill was discreetly presented to her in a fake leather folder. She paid it and left a generous tip. As she walked away from the table, already the waitress was moving in to clear away the cup and plates. Would she notice? No, don't run – she forced herself to walk at normal speed, breathing deeply, somewhere between elation and terror. Across the lobby, then into the revolving door. If it's to happen, it'll happen now . . .

Nothing.

The rain had stopped, but it was still cold. She crossed the road and went into Stephen's Green. She felt good now: better than she'd done in months. She felt so good that she took the handbag back to the shop that afternoon and got a credit note for it. She went home on the train, and told Kevin she'd had a good time in town.

'Didn't buy anything, though.'

The spoon was special. Everything after that had been an attempt to replicate the feeling she experienced when she walked out of the Shelbourne with it in her pocket. Looking at it she remembered the feeling, but only as one remembers pain or ecstasy: the fact of it, but not the thing itself. Of course it had never been the same again. Kevin would be so upset if he knew she still had the spoon . . .

She heard the door of the studio slam, and she hurried to put the spoon back in its hiding place. Kevin had wanted to tell Claire, but she said that if he did, she wouldn't go to Donegal. Claire was so different, she wouldn't understand. But then again, Nuala herself still didn't know why she had done what she had.

4

'I HAD YOUR SISTER IN HERE YESTERDAY,' Rita said.
Claire looked at her blankly. She didn't have any sisters.
Rita stared back unblinkingly at her across the counter,
across swiss rolls filled with pineapple jam and packets
of fig rolls. Suddenly Claire realized whom she meant.

'My sister? *She's* not my sister.'

'Isn't she?' said Rita, the spoken query implying the
unspoken one: 'Then who is she?'

'She's my cousin.'

Behind Rita's head, a new blade for a billhook hung
from a nail on the wall. The door behind the counter
which led from the shop into the living room was slightly
ajar. Claire could hear a radio on somewhere out in the
kitchen: a phone-in, mixed with jingles and adverts.
Half heard, it was clear that it had been planned to be
only half listened to. Through the door she could see a
floral carpet and the end of a tweedy sofa. She could
visualize the rest of the room from memory.

You could get everything you needed to keep body
and soul together in Rita's shop: tea and asprin, cigarettes and milk, thick socks, Mars Bars, Tampax, tinned
peas, newspapers. To go into it for the first time, the
range of stock looked eccentric until you actually came to

rely on Rita for things, and then you realized that it was quite sensible and comprehensive. Once, in an art magazine in Germany, Claire had seen a series of photographs of a house and shop in Scotland which looked just like Rita's. She'd been surprised how much it had annoyed her. Had blandness reached such proportions on the Continent that something as simple and real as Rita's shop with its boxes of crisps and sliced loaves, and her front room, with her son's football trophies on the mantelpiece could become objects of fascination and wonder? Claire paid for the things she needed and left the shop. Yes, she'd hated those pictures, but then she'd never had much time for that kind of photograpy, and its endless desire to turn other people's lives, deaths and living rooms into an aesthetic experience. But Claire herself was aware of how she moved in two worlds at once, with less conflict than she would have thought possible. Take Catholic kitsch for example: some people she knew thought it was a serious aid to religious devotion; other friends liked it because it was camp.

That she was an artist and that hers was the most drab house in the neighbourhood was an irony not lost on Claire. When she had been away somewhere for a short while it was always good to come back and crest the rise, to see the houses scattered over the landscape. Apart from the bright blue pub, they had mostly been painted in soft, creamy colours: pink, like a marshmallow, yellow, like a scrambled egg. Where she lived provided ample proof of how colour depended on light. Things could look drab, then suddenly vivid when the sun broke through. Her own house at the end of the headland, was of stern grey stone, the wooden eaves, the window frames and sills painted an unremarkable shade of green.

The house nearest to hers had once been grey too, but had been painted white by its present owner, a Dutch woman named Anna. The first time she visited her, Claire had been disconcerted to find that it was all white on the inside, too. Walls and ceilings, a wooden dresser in the kitchen and the bannister had all been painted white. Claire didn't like it. The absence of colour made her feel uneasy. Anna had shown her around the house with enormous pride. She had been an interior designer back in Holland until her retirement some three years earlier, and had created what she considered to be the perfect Irish country house. Claire wondered if Anna had noticed how unlike other houses in the area it was: Claire's own, for example, with its fruit and vegetable wallpaper and semi-collapsed sofa in the kitchen. But was that a fair comparison? Claire was renting her house, and nothing had been done to it for years, whereas most of her neighbours took more pride in their homes.

Out of curiosity, Claire had pressed Anna to tell her what she disliked about Donegal, but the Dutch woman was tactful to a fault, and would make no criticisms. Only when Claire persisted did she say reluctantly, 'Well, this is my professional self coming out, but I do think some of the new houses here are quite ugly.'

'Bungalow blight, it's called,' Claire said. There were no new houses in the immediate vicinity as no one wanted to build in such a remote place, but there were plenty of bungalows near the town. Suddenly Anna dropped her guard.

'I cannot understand why the government allows people to build such ugly houses. They would look hideous no matter where they were, but to see them ruining such a magnificent landscape makes me want to weep. I tell you, Claire, it is a national tragedy, and the people just don't seem to realize that it's happening.'

Claire didn't argue with her, but she thought Anna was missing the point her own mother had made when Claire herself fulminated against the bungalows.

'You only think that because you have a choice,' she said firmly. 'We've given you a good education, you've had a chance to travel and see things and you've decided to come back to Donegal and live simply. But most of the people here have had different lives, and they've chosen differently. They grew up in hardship and now when they can have comfort and luxury, they want it, and who's to blame them for that? Maybe you don't like their cabinets full of Waterford Glass and their chandeliers, but they do.' Claire remembered this when Anna delightedly showed her the antique butter-making equipment she had recently bought: butter pats, stamps, a wooden bowl.

Anna had bought her house some years back from a German family, who had sold up at the end of their second summer there. The purchase had been a mistake, something they readily admitted, even though they liked Donegal. The problem was that they had simply underestimated the place, particularly its weather and isolation. Only after they had done it once did they fully appreciate the difficult logistics involved in getting a car and two tiny children and all the things they considered necessary for a summer across a large tract of Europe and two stretches of water. Claire heard through Rita that they had bought a holiday home in Italy with the money they got when they sold the house to Anna.

Anna also brought her car over from the Continent every summer, but didn't seem to consider it too troublesome. She remarked that it was the price to be paid for coming to such a place. If it had been more easily accessible, then it would have been overrun and spoilt long since, losing the emptiness which was, for her, a special part of its charm.

Claire had always found Anna to be exceptionally reserved, and even though they now knew each other well, she still knew precious little about her life back in Holland. For a long time Claire had assumed she was divorced, but then Anna told her that her husband was dead. She once mentioned a grown-up daughter, but never talked about her. Claire wasn't convinced that she was suited to living on her own, no matter how much Anna protested that she loved it. She struck Claire as someone who needed company, and fortunately she was popular locally, fitting in exceptionally well there. Rita was one of her best friends, a fact which baffled Claire.

As she walked back from Rita's shop that morning, she wasn't surprised to see, when she was still some distance from it, the door of Anna's house open and Nuala emerge. In the short time she had been there, Nuala had already become fast friends with the older woman. Claire had known that it would be so: even before Nuala's arrival she had rung Anna to ask if her cousin might call to visit her. She phrased it as though she were asking a favour, but knew that she was really doing Anna a kindness, and this was confirmed in the delight with which she spoke to Claire after Nuala's first visit.

'And she's to stay for the whole summer?' Anna asked.

'That's the idea, anyway,' Claire replied.

'But why is she here?' asked Anna, suddenly shrewd.

'Oh, you'll have to find that out for yourself,' Claire said.

For her part, Nuala also announced herself well pleased with her new friend, returning to Claire's house with a stack of glossy French and Italian interior design magazines and a wedge of home-made cake. The only problem had arisen from Anna's interest in Nuala's name.

'It was so embarrassing,' Nuala said. 'She started talking about the Children of Lir, and I was racking my brains trying to remember the story. I haven't even thought about it since I was a kid, but she knew it chapter and verse.'

'What Anna doesn't know about Irish customs and mythology isn't worth knowing,' Claire told her. 'She's even been teaching herself to read Irish.'

Never in all her life had Claire seen as slow a walker as Nuala. The two of them had attempted to go for a walk together at the weekend, but it hadn't been a success. She realized now what a mistake it had been: although maybe she had been the one who was at fault, in expecting too much. Nuala had been amazed and appalled by the distance Claire had expected her to cover, something Claire had been able to tell even before they left the house. The seriousness of the preparations, with their emphasis on thick socks and waterproof clothing, clearly alarmed Nuala, although she tried not to show it. Once they got out on to the hills, Claire was exasperated, in spite of herself, by Nuala's slowness and lack of energy. The expedition didn't last long, and before they were home, Claire was silently vowing not to repeat the experience for the rest of the summer.

As they walked back to the house now, Claire had to slow down almost to a standstill so as not to catch up with her dawdling guest. She was avoiding her simply because they spent so much time together as it was. For all that, she wasn't finding Nuala's presence as tiresome as she had feared it might be.

The first couple of days she had found eerie. Nuala looked exactly like Claire's childhood memories of Auntie Kate. It wasn't just that she had exactly the same small stature, round blue eyes and general air of glossy well-being as her mother. She had all her mannerisms too, the same inflections of voice and turns of phrase, and given Auntie Kate was now almost a year dead, Claire couldn't help finding it slightly creepy.

A routine had quickly been established. Every morning, after breakfast, Claire would go to her studio, while Nuala walked down to Rita's shop and bought a newspaper. On returning to the house, she would spend the remainder of the forenoon reading the paper and drinking tea, until it was time for her to begin preparing lunch. She had insisted on doing the cooking while she was there, but brushed off any compliments Claire made about the meals she prepared.

'You must be kidding. Kevin's a far better cook than I am, he never even lets me cook at home. I know you may find this hard to believe, but I'm not really very interested in food. I have to pretend, of course, because of the restaurant. It wouldn't do for the image. I look after the money side of the business, and Kevin and the chef take everything to do with the menu planning. But because we run it together I have to play the part when journalists come to do features for the food pages. I always think it's such a hoot afterwards, they write guff like, "Kevin and Nuala care passionately about wild berries." Of course we clip the article and put it in the window, and you wouldn't believe how things like that draw people in. Anyway, I probably shouldn't be telling you this. Kevin gets really upset if I make jokes about it to anyone in Dublin. He's afraid it'll get about and people will think we're cynical, and that it'll ruin the business. As if I'd be so foolish as to let a thing like that happen!'

Claire wasn't as surprised by this as Nuala might have expected, for she had already noticed her indifference to food, how she was even given to eating things like Mars Bars – two at a sitting – or sickly sweet cakes from Rita's shop.

'Mind you,' Nuala had added, 'it was my idea that we open an Irish restaurant. Kevin wanted it to be an Italian place, but I said no. Told him we wouldn't last six months if we did that. Bacon and cabbage, colcannon, boxty, things like that I told him, but he thought I was being really cynical. "You mean a restaurant for tourists?" he said to me. "A good restaurant," I said. I knew that if we offered the very best of Irish food, traditional dishes cooked to perfection, good bread, fish, beautifully served, that we would do well. "We'll get everyone," I said to him. "Tourists, locals, the lot." And I was right, of course.'

After dinner, sitting by the fire, Nuala would sometimes remind Nuala of an animal moulting. She emanated that same air of glumness, of knowing that there was something amiss, while not quite knowing what it was. Claire was tempted to say to her, 'It's called life, Nuala, and you'd better get used to it,' but she didn't because she knew that Nuala wouldn't understand. This was something she would have to work through for herself, and she could have done a lot worse than come to Donegal to do it.

5

IT UPSET HER out of all proportion when she awoke one morning around dawn, and couldn't remember where she was. One side of the bed was against the wall, and where was Kevin? Blankets rather than a quilt, the room had a wooden ceiling . . .

Nuala realized instantaneously that she was in Claire's house, but that was little consolation. The outstanding question remained: *Why* was she here? And why had the oddness of it not struck her until now?

Things were no clearer later that day, when she sat on the beach below Claire's house, in a relatively secluded and sheltered spot behind some rocks. Moodily she took up handfuls of sand, let it run through her fingers, took up more sand, and again let it scatter. Out in the bay there were five large dark birds sitting on an outcrop of rock. She'd seen them there a few days earlier, and described them to Claire, who had told her what they were called. But Nuala had already forgotten the name Claire had given them.

Why was she here? It baffled her, and that was the only thing that consoled her. Bafflement had become her natural state over the past year, so that it no longer upset her that she didn't have ready answers for everything.

Truer to say that she didn't have answers for anything now. To all Kevin's questions, to her father, the doctor, to those few people who had been close enough to know that something was wrong and asked her what it was, she had only been able to answer, 'I don't know.' She had been afraid to tell them just how confused she was.

Baffled was the word she had used to the doctor who asked her if she was depressed. 'Oh no,' she'd replied. 'Just baffled. Absolutely baffled.'

'About what?'

'Everything. The only thing I'm certain about is that I'm confused.' And confusion was exhausting. It had been her own decision to come to Donegal. She didn't know if it would help, but thought it might eliminate some of the questions that troubled her. In that, she had been right. Being around Anna and Claire was proving to be less puzzling than being with Kevin and the baby.

It had been her birthday in May, not long before Kevin found out what she had been up to. He asked the chef in the restaurant to bake a cake for her, with a ribbon on it, and candles.

'I wasn't sure if I ought to do this,' he said. 'Maybe you won't feel like celebrating.'

She'd spent her birthday last year with her mother. It had fallen on a Saturday, and all four of them had gone out to Wicklow and had lunch in a hotel there. She'd announced to her parents that she was expecting a baby. She'd known for some time, but had saved up the news to tell them. Her mother had been every bit as delighted as Nuala thought she would be, and in the week after that she was already giving her advice and wanting to

36

help her buy the things she would need. The following Saturday, her mother died.

Grief wasn't the half of it. It triggered in her a loss of confidence, as if she'd woken up in the middle of life, not knowing how she'd got there. When the baby was born in the autumn, she'd been ashamed to tell anyone how disappointed she was. She kept her feelings hidden from everyone, even from Kevin, allowing herself to manifest only the emotions she thought would be fitting.

She'd become obsessed with the idea that she hadn't known her mother as well as she ought to have done. She'd known her as a mother, but had never seen her as a woman in her own right. Would her own child ever really know her? Nuala did love her baby, but right from the moment it was born its separateness from her both fascinated and appalled. How well, she wondered, did she know her own husband?

One day in February, Kevin had remarked that B.B. King was coming to Dublin, and he was hoping to go to hear him. 'But you don't like jazz.'

'Yes I do,' he said.

'But I didn't know you liked B.B. King. You don't have any of his records.'

'Actually, I do.'

'But you never listen to them.'

'God Nuala, do I have to be a fully paid-up member of his fan club before I can go to one of his concerts? I thought it would be a good night out, why do you have to make such a big deal about it?'

Another time, Reykjavik was mentioned on television, and Kevin said casually, 'I was there once.'

'What? You never told me you'd been to Iceland.'

'Well, can you really call three hours in the transit lounge of Keflavik airport "being in Iceland"?' Apparently, Nuala could.

'I can't believe I've known you all these years and you never told me that!'

'But what was there to tell? A refuelling stop on a cheap flight to the States when I was a student: do you really want to know about that?'

'Yes,' she said. 'What else are you keeping from me?'

'Well,' he said, 'did I ever tell you that when I was five I had a hamster called Jerry?'

'No Kevin,' Nuala said plaintively. 'You never told me that either.'

Kevin stared at her. 'What's got into you at all, Nuala? That was a joke. I mean, none of this stuff matters a damn.'

'It matters to me,' she said. 'You're my husband, I ought to know you.' Over the following weeks she continued to pester him with questions which even she knew were trivial. She also asked her father to tell her every last thing he could remember about her mother, and it had made him so uneasy that he mentioned it to Kevin.

She looked at strangers, too, and wondered about their lives. Nuala had wide blue eyes and a frank stare which was more disconcerting than she realized. A man in a red Porsche drew up beside her at a traffic light one afternoon. She gazed over, wondering how much it meant to him to have a car like that. And what real difference did it make anyway? The man saw her looking at him, and drew the wrong conclusion. He leered over

38

at her, and mouthed a silent obscenity. Nuala grinned back nastily, and drew her index finger across her throat. Whatever reaction he had expected, it wasn't that. The lights changed, and she roared away.

At night, she would sit in the restaurant at a table near the kitchen door, and would surreptitiously gaze at the guests enjoying their meals. A sort of innocence she thought, fell over people when their food was set in front of them and they started to eat: they became like little children. How did it all connect? There was a woman in a short skirt which was fashionable, but looked absurd on her. Why couldn't she see that? The elegance of the room, the frail tinkling sounds of cutlery and conversation: and behind the kitchen door, the hot, muffled pandemonium of the kitchen. How did they keep up the pretence? Or did they just not know? One night a woman looked up suddenly while Nuala was staring at her, and each met the other's gaze. They looked at each other for some moments, then Nuala slowly shook her head. A look of desperation flickered on the woman's face, then she shrugged and looked away, picked up her wine glass and pretended to join in the conversation. Nuala was sorry she had no answers to give her.

Shortly after had come the spending sprees, and then she had started to take things. Even now, months later, Nuala couldn't bring herself to call it stealing, because that would make her a thief, and that was inconceivable. A thief was someone who got into someone else's car and drove off, or put their hand in your pocket and took your credit cards, or broke into other people's houses and took their jewellery and hi-fi. She never took from shops. That would have been wrong. Not only did

Nuala not want the things she took: she didn't see how anyone else could possibly want them or place any value on them. First, there was the teaspoon from the hotel. Then more spoons. Promotional ashtrays: a red plastic one with the words 'Enjoy the real thing' and the Coca-Cola logo on it in white. Three pins for holding corn on the cob while you ate it. (Three! What more proof could anyone want that she hadn't been serious about any of this.) A pottery bowl full of packets of sugar and sweeteners. And then there was the teapot.

'I got it in the Kilkenny Design Centre,' she said bleakly to Kevin.

'Got it? You mean that's where you took it from,' he replied pitilessly. 'It may have escaped your notice, but you can buy teapots in the Kilkenny Design Centre. Dozens of them. All for sale, matching cups and saucers if you want them.'

'I know that.'

'Then why did you steal it?'

Nuala didn't know. She only knew that it had been a mistake. The teapot, which she'd taken from the upstairs café, was too big. She'd noticed a woman at the next table drop her mouthful of cheesecake from her fork and stare in shock as she watched Nuala brazenly cram the teapot into her handbag. She zipped it closed and scowled at the woman, hoping that what she was seeing would be so extraordinary that the woman would literally not believe her eyes, and not report her. She couldn't take any chances, and left at once. It had annoyed her to have someone gawping at her just at the moment she was discovering a teapot could not be slipped into your bag with the ease and speed that you could get rid of a spoon or an ashtray, particulary when the teapot is hot, and still has tea in it. More tea than she had imagined: as she walked down Nassau Street she could feel the hot liquid seeping through her bag, against her hip. When she got home it took her a long time to clear up the mess. There were tea-leaves in her address book, her diary, everywhere. Grimly picking damp tea-leaves out of her hairbrush, she knew that she had come to the end of something.

So she took the teapot down to the kitchen and set it on the table, and she brought down all the other things from their hiding places, and set them out too. There were more things than she had thought there would be.

'Where did all this stuff come from?' Kevin asked when he came in.

'Oh, different places. I didn't buy any of it,' she said pointedly, and she watched him as his puzzlement gave way to realization and then to shock. She started the conversation feeling distant, as though all this were happening to someone else, and ended up wishing that it were so.

Within a week, she was in Donegal. The night before she left, she'd closed herself away and looked at every photo she had of herself: pictures of her wedding day, holiday snapshots, school photos. She looked out at herself from all of them, blank and cheerful. None of them gave her the answer she required, and so she turned to things which belonged to her, some precious, some trivial: a key fob with keys to the house, the car, the restaurant; the opal pendant Kevin had given her the first Christmas after they were married, a pair of espadrilles she'd bought in Crete two summers earlier. She held these things in her hands, wanting to wrest from them the energies they held, the energies she had put into them by possessing them.

Nothing.

She came out of the room and said to Kevin, 'You mustn't ever think that I don't love you, because I do.'

What *were* those birds called? Cormorants. Yes, that was it, cormorants.

Was she there just to punish herself? For it was punishment, she dared not think how much she missed Kevin and the baby, how much she missed being at home.

'Do you know exactly why I'm here?' she had asked Claire at breakfast that morning.

'I think I do,' Claire replied carefully.

'Does it bother you?'

'Not in the least. Why should it? Most people have a crisis in their lives at one time or another. You might as well have yours now, get it over and done with early, so that you can get on with the rest of your life in peace. Not that you have any real choice in the matter. These things take their course, but they do pass. It's hard to believe at the time, but it will come to an end.'

Nuala was grateful for this, and for the casual tone in which Claire spoke these words, but she didn't know what to say in reply, so she just nodded firmly, and went on eating.

The cormorants had flown away now, but further along the beach there was a gaggle of small dark birds with spindly red legs. She didn't know what they were called either, and frankly admitted to herself that she didn't care. Before coming here, she had never realized there were so very many different types of birds, and secretly she wondered what point there was to it. Whole species could have vanished overnight, and she would never have missed them. And Kevin was even worse than Nuala in this respect. He wouldn't have lasted a week here, never mind a summer.

She pulled a bar of chocolate out of her pocket, and ate it absent-mindedly. Sea air gave you an appetite, she thought. It grew colder, and she felt a few drops of rain on her face. Forget the birds: she hadn't known there were so many different types of rain until she arrived in Donegal. The kind she liked least was the fine mist, almost invisible, that could leave you much wetter than a solid, honest downpour. Claire had asked her to bring back anything interesting she found on the beach.

'Such as?' Nuala had asked.

'Sea glass,' Claire said. 'Bits of pottery. Shells, or pieces of driftwood, but only if they're particularly interesting.' There were a few bits of wood, but Nuala thought even Claire would have had to admit they all looked boring. Could a piece of wood that had been floating around in the sea be interesting? She did find a fragment of pottery, though. You always found bits of plate on the beach. Where on earth did they come from? Did so many people have picnics at the beach with proper plates, and did they always come to grief? Did sailors do their washing up over the sides of boats, and did the greasy crockery often slip from their fingers, to be smashed on the rocks and washed up on beaches like this? There had to be a reason. Maybe she would ask Claire, she might know. The rain was getting heavier now: she got up , shook herself, and turned towards the path back to the house.

6

WHEN YOU CONSIDER a work of art, size matters. Claire was interested in how the dimensions of a painting or sculpture influenced one's reaction to it. When she was working, she found that she didn't have to decide consciously how big or small a painting should be. That was one aspect which had never given her significant problems. She thought it absurd how slides were used to teach art appreciation, not least because it gave the impression that all paintings were the same size. The sense of scale was lost. When she visited art galleries, pictures which she had seen reproduced in books would often turn out to be much larger or smaller than she had imagined they would be, and she often revised her opinion of them when confronted with the original.

For some painters, it was more of a problem, more of an issue. Alice had been interested in working on a massive scale, but it hadn't been easy. Her studio was too small, and the materials were expensive. She had been enraged when people had tried to discourage her by saying it would be better to work on smaller canvases, because no one would want to exhibit, much less buy, such huge paintings. She knew what they had in mind: something which would fit comfortably over a mantelpiece.

There were paintings whose impact depended simply on their being big, such as Warhol's portrait of Mao. What interested Claire more were such things as Egyptian statues, massive and affecting; or the powerful energies which emanate from tiny Etruscan bronzes. There could be prejudice against a work simply because it was small. Between the wars, Giacometti worked on sculptures of heads which became progressively smaller and smaller until each one was no bigger than a pea, and he was able to carry the work of several years around with him in a large matchbox. Because of this, hardly anyone would take him seriously as an artist.

Size. And essence. Essence of the subject. Of the material used. Wood different to stone. Stone different to metal. Each metal, each wood, each type of stone different. These materials different collectively to paint, and then in turn, each type of paint having its own resonance. Gauguin. Rough, open-weave canvas transported specially from Paris to the islands of Polynesia, to give his paintings the primitive air he desired. Oils. Acrylics. Too plastic for me, Claire thought, too shiny, the colours garish, difficult to mute. Fine, if that's what you want. You need new materials to express new realities, just as you need new forms. How to combine the material, the form and the consciousness, that was what it was about. That was why she knew better than to give serious attention to figurative watercolours of landscapes. She was interested in the idea of combining forms and materials which seemed inexorably opposed to each other. The idea of a portrait in pastels which would be completely contemporary appealed to her, but her attempts to execute such a work had never satisfied her.

45

She thought a lot about these ideas because she wasn't happy with her work, and wanted to push through on to a new level. She knew, though, that progress would be made only through the work itself, not by thinking about it. But her mind was scattered. In recent weeks, she had found it hard to concentrate.

She thought about Nuala. Her otherness. That was what was interesting about it, and provided a suitable distraction for Claire. She would encourage Nuala to go out, and from the window of the studio she would watch her walk away from the house. Claire liked looking at people when they didn't realize it, when they weren't looking at her. Not that she was a voyeur: she didn't want to spy on them when they were doing something which would be generally accepted as private. She just liked to look at a subject without the subject looking back at her. Once she had made a series of paintings which she liked to think of as portraits. They were views of the backs of people's heads. She liked them because she thought you could actually tell more about a person viewing them in such a way than if you looked them in the face. Faces can deceive. Claire didn't think there was anything at all anonymous about the back view of a person. You were seeing them as they would never see themselves.

Nuala's room. 'It is in my house,' Claire thought, 'but it is different now, because she is there.' Her things. Yes, Claire would stand by the window and watch until Nuala reached the bottom of the lane, when she would either turn right to go to Anna's house, or left to go down to the sea. Then Claire would leave the studio and go into Nuala's room.

At first she was timid, and would confine herself to standing at the door, looking in. Clothes on the back of a chair. Open suitcase. Scattered shoes. Cosmetic bottles on the dressing table. A soft black brush with a wooden handle, for applying face powder.

As time passed, she got bolder. After a few days, she would go right into the room, and soon she was looking freely at everything, touching and appraising objects. She even slipped her feet into a pair of shoes one day. (They turned out to be much too big for Claire, which surprised her.) She was always careful to leave everything in the same apparently random position she had found it, for it would have been embarrassing had Nuala realized what she was doing. There was a bottle of perfume. Paloma Picasso. Claire smiled when she saw that. She took the lid off and sniffed; would have liked to spray some on her wrist, but that would have been too risky. A toy rabbit. A diary. It never entered Claire's mind to open it and read it. Whatever she was looking for in Nuala's room, it wasn't the sort of knowledge she would find there.

It would have been hard for Claire to explain what she felt, looking around that austere room, and she wondered how Nuala saw it. How to express or explain that strange combination of longing and mystery she found in other people's possessions, and which she suspected had something to do simply with the fact that they belonged to other people? And it wasn't just the objects themselves, it was the whole atmosphere of the abandoned room, which another person had just left. What did all these things mean to Nuala? Some of them she would have considered insignificant, others would have

47

been of great importance to her. Claire suspected that the cloth rabbit probably fell in the latter category.

She picked it up and sniffed it. The sense of smell is greatly underrated. The rabbit gave off that musty, milky smell of babies or very small children. It was a bit grubby, but intact: no ripped ears or missing tail. It was evident that the child to whom it belonged loved it very much, perhaps it was her favourite toy. Claire imagined that Nuala's little girl was the most important person in her life, that she probably loved her as she had never loved anyone else. Sometimes she would think of how, in the past, she would not have believed such a love to be possible. Such concern for her. She's delicate. Perhaps. Vulnerable. But she would also remember how much she meant to her, and somehow this small-ness and importance would seem incompatible. It would be frightening to have one's whole life fixed upon so small a point. What would she do if she wasn't there? She'd be lost without her. Her sense of herself would have no centre, she would be adrift. The more she cherished her the more this feeling would grow. Claire imagined Nuala creeping into the nursery at night to look at her while she slept. She would do this to check on her, to make sure that she was still breath-ing. Leaning over the cot, gently, so as not to wake her she would pick the cloth rabbit up by the ear, and look at it. The cloth rabbit, having no choice because of its fixed stare, looks straight back, and the very smallness of the rabbit would make anyone want to weep. Because size, you see, is important. How we react to things is often triggered principally by the dimensions of the object . . .

'Did you bring any photographs of the baby with you?'

'Yes, of course. Would you like to see them?'

'Very much.'

Nuala went to her room, and brought down an envelope of photos, which she poured over the sofa. 'They're all mixed up. I just put them in at the last minute. Look, this one was taken in the hospital, the day after she was born.' There were others that had been taken in Kevin's and Nuala's house in Monkstown, and looking at them, Claire was more aware than ever of how spartan and uncomfortable her own home must have seemed to Nuala.

'Look at us,' Nuala said, passing Claire a photo of herself with Kevin and the baby. 'We look like we're advertising life insurance.' Claire was taken aback both by the remark itself and the coldness of her tone.

'I haven't looked at these since I got here,' Nuala said, staring hard at another picture. 'It feels funny looking at them, it seems like such a long time since I was there, but it's only – what, three weeks now?'

'Yes, just that.'

Nuala picked up another photo of the baby asleep in her cot, and looked at it in silence for a long time. Being so deeply absorbed, she didn't notice how interested Claire was in the photographs where Kevin appeared. They hadn't met since they were at college together, and she was curious to see how much he had changed over the years.

'I do miss them,' Nuala said suddenly.

'I'm sure you do,' Claire said.

'You must believe that. I'd hate it so much if you or anyone thought I was selfish coming away here and leaving them in Dublin, especially the baby. Sometimes I'm really lonely for them.'

'It doesn't matter what I think, or what anybody thinks,' Claire said. 'You have to do what you believe to be right.' Nuala nodded, but looked uneasy.

Claire also felt uncomfortable, because she was afraid that Nuala would start to ask her how she felt about children: Did it bother her that she didn't have any, would she like to have them in the future? She never liked talking about this, but with Nuala, because of who she was married to, she would have found it particularly awkward and embarrassing.

There might well have been a child: she had become pregnant while she was at art school. Nuala didn't know this: almost no one knew. She hadn't even told the man concerned. It was a common enough story: she thought she loved him, but going to bed with him had changed everything. By the time she found out what had happened, she didn't even like him any more. She didn't want to involve him in any decisions she had to make. Above all, she was afraid of them being forced together by a combination of social pressure and circumstance, and it would all end badly, of that she was certain. More than ten years later, sitting in her own kitchen and looking sideways at Nuala frowning with concentration over her photos, she felt completely vindicated in what she had decided to do.

She still didn't like to think back to that time. It was no cliché to say that the first weeks had been a nightmare to her. Part of her reason for not telling anyone had been denial on her part. First there was the hope that she was mistaken, followed by the certainty that she was not, which was coupled with a superstitious and certainly absurd idea that if she didn't tell anyone then it wasn't real, like a child thinking she couldn't be seen when her eyes were closed. But then she started to be sick in the mornings. She was living in a grim bedsitter at that time, where the bathroom was three floors down. Wretched with nausea, she would look out over the roofs and chimneys of the city, and despair of knowing what she should do. Every possible scenario she could imagine seemed ghastly in its own way. She looked around the squalid room, and tried to imagine living there with a baby. What if she had to drop out of art school? That was the last thing she wanted. What was she to do, how was she to make a living for herself and the baby? She would have to do what was best for the child: she accepted responsibility for the situation she was in, but couldn't work out a plan that seemed viable and which would allow her to keep the baby and look after it as it would need to be looked after.

Adoption began to look like the only course open to her. Lots of people who wanted children couldn't have them, people who could give a baby a degree of material comfort she could never hope to provide.

One of the strangest things was that, through all of this, the baby remained an abstraction. She thought of it constantly, but she knew that the reality of it was somehow always eluding her, until one day when she found herself sharing a table in a café with a woman and a baby, and realized that she was staring at it as if this were the very child whose fate she was trying to decide. She thought she'd never before seen such a gorgeous baby, although she was well aware that nature had designed them to look appealing; cuteness was built into them as an evolutionary weapon. Knowing that made no difference: looking at the baby's big soft eyes and wet mouth she thought that it was as wrong to regard the situation in which she now found herself in purely functional and pragmatic terms as it would be to deal with it in a purely emotional way. You had to take them on their own terms, which did involve irrationality and affection. The baby smiled across the table at her. Claire smiled back.

She also took careful note of the woman on whose knees the baby was sitting. Not much older than Claire, she was elegantly dressed, and obviously well off. As the woman spooned pudding into the baby's mouth, Claire gradually realized that without even being aware of it, she had bought society's message: that some women were entitled to have children and some women were not. This woman was one of the former; Claire was not. And this by her own definition! What had she been doing over the past days and weeks but rationalizing herself out of motherhood. When she imagined giving her baby up for adoption, her image of the child had been hazy, while the image she had in mind of the woman who would become the adoptive mother had been consistent and clear: a woman such as this.

Claire had been long enough in Dublin by that time to visualize, with considerable accuracy, the other woman's whole life: her house in the suburbs, the restaurants she ate in, the shops where she bought her clothes, where she went in the summer.

You were supposed to choose: that was the hidden contract. You could have your painting and an austere life, or you could have children. You weren't allowed to have both. 'Who says I can't?' she thought with sudden defiance. She decided there in the café that when the baby was born she would keep it and bring it up herself, no matter how difficult that would be. She'd never really believed that there was such a thing as security anyway, and she felt that in these circumstances this would be helpful to her, and give her strength. The last thing she needed at such a time was delusion.

Her mind had been quite made up. She would always remember the weeks which followed as calm and contented, as she settled down with the decision she'd made. It was early summer. College ended for the holidays, but Claire stayed on in Dublin, which was undergoing a heatwave. She felt more nauseous than ever, and the sweltering weather made it worse, but she felt peaceful and happy for all that.

She lost the baby in the fourth month of her pregnancy. It happened at home: she'd finally gone there to explain the situation to her parents. It was all over even before she had had time to tell them. Her mother cried but she didn't reproach her, as Claire had been afraid she might.

'How could I blame you?' her mother had said, 'when exactly the same thing happened to me?'

What happened to her mother had been worse. She was only fifteen at the time, and when her father found out, he'd beaten her so hard she lost the baby at once. The family hushed it up. Her father told her he'd beat her again, that he'd throw her out of the house if word got around the neighbourhood about what had happened.

'I hated men after that,' Claire's mother said frankly. 'They'd brought me only trouble and sorrow, and I wanted nothing more to do with them. I was going to be my own woman. It was fifteen years before I could trust a man again, and even then it wasn't easy.'

She'd been thirty when she met Claire's father. 'I got fond of him, in spite of myself. I loved him, but I was afraid. He wouldn't take no for an answer. In the end, I went away to Galway, but he came after me. Said he'd keep coming after me, wherever I went. But he made me a promise. He said if we got married and I went away after that, then he'd leave me in peace. "What sort of promise do you call that?" I asked him. "It's a promise that if you marry me, you'll always be free," he said. So I married him, and I've always been glad that I did.'

'Why didn't you tell me all this sooner?' Claire asked.

'Same reason, I suppose, that you're only telling me now, when it's late in the day, and the horse has bolted. I'm still ashamed of it. Just think. All those years ago, and I'm still ashamed.'

Claire had spent the rest of that summer at home in Donegal, and when she went back to Dublin in the autumn she moved into a different flat. It was no more appealing than the one in which she had previously been living: the only thing in its favour was freedom from the associations and memories of that time. She didn't tell any of her friends, although she suspected that Alice guessed what had happened, but was good enough not to ask for confirmation or denial. Unlike her mother, Claire didn't feel ashamed, but her mother's story was such a significant part of the whole experience that she felt the only option could be silence. It troubled

Claire that had she not got pregnant, that side of her mother's life would always have remained shut to her. People might often unwittingly remind her of what had happened (as was the case this evening), but other than that, no one had ever been able wilfully to bring up the subject and attempt to reproach her with it.

Years later, what was the net result? It left her a fatalist. She would wince to hear people talk about what they wanted to happen in life, foolishly confident that they knew their own best interests; worse, that they could have whatever they wanted by effort of will.

She hadn't ruled out having children in the future, nor dismissed the possibility of spending her life with one particular person. These things had not yet happened, there was no way of knowing whether or not they would happen, but trying to wring out one's own destiny was doomed, of that she was convinced.

But fatalism was no insulation against hurt. Claire still felt sad when she thought of the baby. To think 'what if?' was permissible, never 'if only . . .'

Still, her sense of irony had not been diminished by life's vicissitudes, so she was able to appreciate Nuala's presence in the house. Nuala had noticed that Claire wasn't really paying attention to the photographs after a certain point, but it didn't bother her. Suddenly she realized that one of the things she liked most about Claire was that she wasn't judgemental, and how rare that was. She wanted to tell her, but when Claire looked her in the eye, she faltered, and said something else instead.

7

ONE NIGHT IN JULY, Claire found that she couldn't get to
sleep, even though she had worked hard during the day
and was tired. She put it down to there being a full
moon. The moon always made her think of her father,
the most superstitious person she had ever known. On a
night such as this, he would always go outside and turn
his money over in his pocket, in the hope that it would
double. Once, years ago, he had discovered he was ten
pounds short of what he should have had, and the
whole family had been enlisted to help him look for it.
Only after every possibility had been considered without
result did he remember that two nights before that, the
moon had been full. Shamefacedly, he admitted that in
turning the money over, he must have inadvertently
pulled the note out of his pocket, and lost it to a gust of
wind. Over the years it had become a family joke, but
Claire could still remember how annoyed her mother
had been at the time. 'Maybe that'll put the pagan
practices out of you,' she'd said, (which of course it
didn't). Not that Claire's mother was herself free of such
superstition: she wouldn't allow whitethorn in the
house, and couldn't bear to see shoes on the table. Claire
had picked up these taboos from example, and it made

her feel uneasy to see other people break them.

Anna had taken a keen interest in all this when she talked to her about it once. Claire didn't understand her neighbour's attitude, which combined fascination in these things with the most rational, unmystical cast of mind Claire had ever come across.

She was quite enjoying having Nuala to stay. She liked the company, but until her arrival now almost a month ago, Claire hadn't considered that she lacked companionship. She felt Nuala didn't merit the interest she was taking in her. Markus would have said that it showed there was too little going on in her life, and that she just hadn't realized it until then. But of course Markus would never have seen her choosing to live in such a quiet place as anything other than folly. He'd once spent a year in a remote corner of France, much as she was doing now, living alone and painting. 'Never again,' he said afterwards. 'From now on, I'm only ever going to live in big cities. I find my level of vitality rises or falls to meet the level of vitality of the place where I happen to be.' He'd spent time in Paris after that, and he'd been happy there. Claire didn't agree with what he said. She thought it wasn't true as a general rule, although it was probably true for Markus. But then, that had always been part of the problem: he always had to be doing. Markus had never understood the value of passivity, much less laziness.

Sometimes she wondered if Nuala understood anything else. Before her arrival, Claire had been worried that she would be bored in the country. Now that she was installed in the house, Claire was amazed that the tedium didn't get to her, but it didn't appear to bother

her in the slightest. She spent more time reading the papers every day than Claire would have thought possible: even old papers from under the stairs. 'It's all news, isn't it?' she would say, settling down. 'Just because something terrible happened a month ago, or even years ago, doesn't mean that it deserves less attention than something that happened yesterday.'

Washing newsprint off her hands before beginning to prepare lunch she said one day, 'I always think it's right, somehow, that you're filthy by the time you've finished reading the paper. I always feel grimy inside, so why not outside too?'

Another day she remarked casually, 'The difference between papers and magazines is that they're both like mirrors, but only one of them flatters you when you look into it.' Claire knew what she meant, but pretended she didn't, because she was interested to know how Nuala would explain it.

'Well, look at it this way: there was a piece in the paper yesterday about a woman who had a neurosis about touching things when she was out. She felt she had to buy everything she touched in shops, and it was in the paper because she got into trouble with debt. Bought all sorts of things she didn't want and couldn't afford. Now, that's a very rare problem, but I bet lots of people know at least the germ of the feeling behind that. In magazines you get the idea that everybody is, or could be, perfect, but in papers you get the sense that everybody is at least slightly mad. And sometimes that can be a comfort, because you see you're not the only one. You know, Claire, people are afraid of the most everyday things, but they're too ashamed to admit it. A friend of mine confided in me that she's afraid of going to the hairdresser's. She'll go to the dentist without a second thought, but has to steel herself for days to get her hair cut. After she told me I thought about it, and I watched people, and I came to the conclusion that there's nothing so mundane that someone, somewhere, doesn't feel uneasy about it. Things like using the telephone, even. Or eating out. I see it in the restaurant quite often. But we all go around thinking everyone is more confident than we are, and that no one else knows what it's like to feel insecure or ill at ease with some everyday thing.'

It wasn't a consolation to Claire to think about this: the idea stuck in her mind like a hook, making her think of her own inadequacies. That might be constructive during the day, but fatal when lying awake at two in the morning, and she tried frantically to get her mind on to another track.

Painting. Think of her work, yes, think of that. She was glad she was a painter, she'd rather be that than anything else, no matter that it brought her up frequently, painfully, against her own limitations. Sometimes people said painting had come to the end of its natural life. Sometimes she believed them. Strangely enough, this did not make an enormous difference to her. Claire's father had been a devout Catholic, and once when she was in her teens, she'd asked him, teasing but genuinely curious too, 'What would you do if somebody proved to you that there's no God? I mean, beyond any doubt?'

'Ah, it wouldn't make much odds,' he'd replied mildly. 'I wouldn't let it keep me from Mass of a Sunday, whatever else.' Claire's own dedication to painting was something in the order of this line of reasoning.

Her exchanges with Markus on the subject had always been interesting, not least because there was almost nothing on which they agreed. He used to lament being a sculptor, and insist that the visual arts were inferior to literature. In reply, she would accuse him of despising his own gifts. Images could never have the precision of language, that had been his main argument. That was what she disliked about words, she thought they lacked subtlety. She refused to believe that by writing about apples you could ever say much about things that weren't apples, but when you looked at a Cézanne painting of a bowl of fruit, it expressed knowledge of other things – mortality, tenderness, beauty – in a way that was only possible without words. Markus claimed this was pure emotionalism.

'You only think that because you're afraid of your emotions,' she'd replied.

'Better that than be a slave to them,' he said.

'You must respond to art with your nerves and your heart,' she insisted. 'When you look at a painting, you should *feel* something. If not, then there's something amiss.'

She wondered what he would think of the work she was doing now, so different to what she had been doing when she knew him. She thought he would like it. People used to say to Claire that she had 'mellowed' since college. It used to annoy her, for she didn't believe that it was meant as a compliment, and suspected it was just a sly accusation of softness and loss of energy. She had certainly changed, though, that she would never have denied. Alice had been largely responsible for that, just through Claire having known her.

It hadn't been an easy friendship. Lots of other students had found it impossible to get along with Alice, she'd been so frank and direct. Claire had admired her even when she hadn't always agreed with her, or even liked her. Alice might have been hard on other people, but she was harder still on herself. Her aesthetics and morality, her political and religious views were all carefully thought through and were not open to compromise. The idea of saying something just to please someone else, or to spare their feelings would have struck her as bizarre. Holding an opinion simply because it was in vogue was unthinkable. It was only by knowing someone of such relentless integrity that Claire had come to learn how rare a thing it was, and how often social pressure influenced not only what people said, but even what they thought. She realized that she, too, often went with the prevailing opinions through lazy-mindedness, or worse, want of courage. And courage was something Alice had never lacked. She was, without doubt, the bravest person Claire had ever known, and she'd had a relish for life that Claire, when she first knew her, had rather resented. No, be honest, she'd been jealous of her, for her wit and energy. And her talent, yes, that above all. Alice had been a confident, gifted painter. Looking at her work in the studio Claire had known Alice was a better painter than she would ever be. She'd felt jealous, and realizing that made her feel small-minded. It was a long time before she could admire her work freely and honestly. She'd bought from her the painting which now hung in her sitting room. Alice said she could have it if she wanted it, but Claire had insisted on paying. She'd taken it everywhere with

61

her, and it was a touchstone from which she could draw strength, and realize the need for compassion.

Alice's background was similar to Claire's, having grown up on a farm in Roscommon, but Claire could never understand how she could have come so far so fast. She seemed to have freed herself from her society at a remarkably early age. Like Claire, she had gone to the local convent school; unlike Claire, her rebellion against the religion she had instilled into her was not just a poorly thought-out reaction against authority, but a considered and deeply held position from which she would not be budged. While Claire thought there could be some value in religious ritual, Alice had dismissed it. 'All or nothing. You're just afraid.' She considered that death was the end, and meant complete annihilation, a view which remained unaltered even when she fell ill and was told that she was going to die. But when Claire talked to their mutual friend Tommy about it after Alice's death, he said, 'Don't ever imagine it was easy for her. Of course she was frightened. She might have liked to think that things could be other than they were, but she didn't believe that it could be so, and she couldn't pretend, simply to comfort someone, least of all herself. What Alice believed was bleak and she felt the bleakness of it, every day, right up to the end.'

What this had challenged in Claire was the thoughtless faithlessness that she had drifted into when she was at school, and the full consequences of which she had never properly thought through. She couldn't fully accept Alice's view of things, but she wasn't clear what a valid alternative might be.

When Alice died, she left strict instructions that she

didn't want a religious funeral, even though it was difficult for her family to accept that. Claire was abroad when Alice died, and when she came back it was important for her to talk to friends like Tommy who had been there with her. He didn't share her view that Alice's integrity could only be admired.

'You might not have thought that if you'd seen her mother at the funeral. It was in Dublin, it had to be, for she'd insisted on being cremated rather than buried, and they don't have the facilities for that down the country. Her mother came to me after and she said, "I still can't believe she's gone, I don't feel I've been to a proper funeral at all. I still haven't had a chance to say goodbye." It bothered her too, that she wouldn't have a special place she could go to, to bring flowers and feel close to Alice. I just thought it was so wrong, Claire. You can be too pure, too high-minded, you know. Sometimes you have to compromise.'

'I still don't think it would have been right to have a Mass for her,' Claire argued. 'She was so at odds with that, so against it, that it just couldn't be right.'

'But Claire,' Tommy replied, 'funerals aren't for the people who've died, they're for the people who are left behind. Haven't you grasped even that much?'

She understood what he meant, but stubbornly refused to yield the point. She wanted to take the strict line on Alice's behalf, and needed to do it for herself, to make what had happened bearable.

Claire had been in Germany when Alice died. She'd been looking forward to seeing her again when she went back, for although she was ill, it was thought she would live for at least another six months. Then Tommy rang to tell her Alice had got much worse quite unexpectedly. He rang again three days later to say it could only be a matter of days. Claire had been with Markus at the time. He encouraged her to go out, not to take her mind off Alice, but just because that was what had been planned for the day, that they would go walking in the mountains.

That afternoon, they came across a tiny church, with a graveyard. Some of the tombs had photographs, from many years earlier. Looking at them, Claire had a creeping horror that Alice was right about death. Claire went into the church, and was aware of the different qualities of silence. Outside, the peace of the mountains was full and inhuman, the more complete for being broken by the sound of the wind and the cries of birds. The silence of the chapel was brittle, unnerving: she wanted to laugh, even while this appalled her. It struck her as a dreadful thing to do. She stayed only for a few moments, in a stillness so complete that she felt she had somehow moved outside time, and this intimation of eternity appalled her.

As they walked back down the valley to the house where they were staying, dusk was falling, and she had never seen the valley look so beautiful. After the sun went down, the colours of the trees and the grass suddenly became more vivid than when the sun shone full upon them. They watched the grey clouds cover the peaks of the mountains, and the clustered villages became crowns of light in the dimness. As they rounded a curve in the path they startled some deer, which ran away and hid, shy and light, running in the dusk. And all the time she was thinking of Alice, of her having to leave life. The full moon shone that night, too. It had been there, blank white during the day, and they watched it fill with silver light as the dusk fell.

Shortly after they got back to the house, Tommy rang to say that Alice had died some hours earlier.

8

LESS THAN A QUARTER of a mile away, Anna was also passing a sleepless night. She went down to the white kitchen and made herself a mug of camomile tea. Herbal teas were one of the few things of which she brought supplies from Holland to Ireland every summer. She sat with her hands around the mug, waiting for the tea to draw and then cool sufficiently for her to drink it. Tonight for some reason the light, straw-like scent which she usually found so soothing made her feel slightly queasy. She was in a worse mood than she had pretended to herself. Acknowledging this, she poured the tea down the sink and made herself a hot whiskey instead.

Anna hated insomnia, which she regarded as one of the most severe penalties of growing old. She had slept so well when she was younger, she remembered Pieter saying to her, 'Sleep is your natural element.' He used to get up in the middle of the night to feed Lili when she cried, and she wouldn't hear him either leaving or returning to the bed. She'd wake in the morning still in a fug of drowsiness for a good hour or so after she got up, as if the night were something she couldn't shake off. It had been particularly hard in Holland where everything started at the crack of dawn; she'd always had to be up so early to get Lili out to school and herself ready for work. When she came to live in Ireland she regretted that she hadn't lived there earlier, for in Donegal nothing much ever happened before ten in the morning. But, as was the case with many things in her life, it was too late by then. Now it took her so long to get to sleep and the slightest sound woke her. Tonight the wind had been blowing about the eaves, but that was nothing new. No, it was her own frame of mind that was keeping her from sleep, and that drove her down to the kitchen and to the whiskey bottle.

To some extent she blamed Nuala, who had called to visit her that afternoon, and confided in her more deeply than ever before mainly on the strength of some Jenever which Anna had rashly produced for her to try, and for which Nuala had instantly developed a great liking. After three glasses she began to tell Anna more about her circumstances than Anna perhaps wished to know, Nuala growing lachrymose and self-pitying in the process.

Ever since her adolescence, people had been confiding in Anna their secrets and problems. Sometimes it puzzled her that this should be so, and she wondered if she was, perhaps, more curious than she cared to admit. Did she, in all honesty, ask leading questions, did she pry? No, she didn't. The irony of it was, Anna herself confided in no one. It wasn't even that she chose not to do so: she really believed that she was incapable of opening her soul to another person. Such secrets as her friends blurted out to her in both Holland and Ireland were mild enough anyway: the familiar litany of

drunken husbands, wayward children, long-held resentments against parents now old and dependent. Rita
once remarked to her, 'It's foolish that you're the only
person around here who I can talk to like this. What do
secrets like mine amount to anyway? There's not a house
round here where you wouldn't hear the same, if they
chose to tell you. If you got every woman in this parish
together and made her write down the thing they were
most ashamed of, and then read them aloud, I bet you'd
have half a dozen women claiming the same story. Oh
yes, we all have our skeletons. Sometimes I wish we had
the courage to bring it all out into the open, to stop
pretending. But we never will.'

By making friends with the local people, Anna felt she
knew and understood more about the area, but in the
mood she was in tonight, she could only see their
confidences as isolating: they trusted her because she
was an outsider. But what did it matter? She loved
Donegal, and never regretted having bought her house
there. She'd loved the place from the moment she
arrived, just after Pieter's death. They'd been living
apart for such a long time, and after all they'd been
through (or rather, after all he'd put her through,) she
hadn't expected that she would be greatly troubled by
his dying. In her worst moments, she'd even thought
that she would feel relieved, that she would be free of
him at last.

But she wasn't relieved. She was devastated. Never
for a moment had she thought they would get back
together again, but she had hoped, even if only in some
vague, half-formed way, that something would be
worked out between them, that some day there would

be some kind of resolution. It didn't happen. If he'd died in the early years of their marriage, just after Lili was born, before all the trouble, then it would have been different. Certainly she would have grieved for him, but it would have been a clean grief. There wouldn't have been this feeling of bitterness, of failure, of unresolved rancour, all of which was compounded by a deep sense of loss. And she hadn't expected to feel like this at all.

She didn't go to the funeral. Lili asked her not to: no, that wasn't true, Lili told her not to go; asked her why she wanted to add hypocrisy to all her other faults and shortcomings. He died in the summer. Anna's best friend Evelien had been about to leave for two weeks' holiday in Ireland, and persuaded her to come too. She had rented a cottage and was going there by car, so there would be no problem in accommodating her.

And so Anna left for Donegal. She had no idea which part of the country that was, for until then, Ireland was a place to which she had given no thought. She was glad that it was, for her, a neutral place. She expected little or nothing from the trip; it was to be nothing more than an escape from a difficult moment in her life.

The only time Anna cried during her first visit to Donegal was on the last day, when she was putting her case on the roof rack of Evelien's car. The thought that she might never see this place again was unbearable to her. They drove off, and at the first town they came to, she asked her friend to stop. 'I'm not going back,' she said. She spent another week in Donegal, and by the end of that time, had entered into negotiations to buy the cottage from the German family.

Her idea at that time was that she would sell up

everything in Holland, and move permanently to Ireland. This had presented practical problems, and by the time they were resolved, she had changed her mind. She was glad now that the plan hadn't worked out, for she knew that it would have been a mistake. She came for Christmas one year, but she didn't enjoy it. It was dark and cold; and she felt isolated and lonely there for the first time ever. As she came to know the place better, she lost some of her illusions about it. There was malice and spite here too, if you cared to see them. It didn't bother her greatly. Anna was more realistic than many visitors, and even felt relieved when she began to catch glimpses of the darker side of life she suspected must be there, for she knew then that she was really getting to know the place in which she had chosen to live. She now came to Ireland every spring, and returned to Holland at the end of the summer. It was a pattern which suited her perfectly.

Sitting tonight in her kitchen, she thought of her apartment back in The Hague. She loved both her houses. She'd been successful in her career as an interior designer and she'd enjoyed it. At least that had worked out. It was some compensation for all the personal unhappiness. Her marriage, her relationship with Lili: sometimes she could be philosophic about this side of her life, shrug, reason that she knew more people whose marriages had failed than had made a success of it. The hidden miseries her Irish neighbours told her were further proof that she was not alone in her unhappiness. But tonight those regrets had the upper hand, and she could do nothing to get them into perspective.

It was three years now since she'd even seen Lili, and

years again since the meeting before that. She'd looked quite different to how Anna had remembered her, looked older than she'd expected, with her hair cropped short in a style that didn't suit her. It was a mild shock to see how much she'd changed, for it brought home to Anna how much of Lili's life had passed in which she had had no part. Not that she wanted to interfere, as Lili claimed, no. She didn't think she had a right to know everything that went on in her daughter's life, but it did hurt to be so completely excluded from it. It wasn't fair for Lili to blame Anna for every failure and lack in her life. It certainly wasn't fair either to hold Anna exclusively responsible for the break up of her marriage to Pieter. That was the heart of the quarrel between Lili and Anna. She wanted to avoid talking about it on this visit, but feared that they would degenerate into wrangling about that very subject.

'I'm so glad to see you again, it's been too long, Lili. You look well,' she lied. 'How do you find me? I must look much older to you.'

'Yes,' said Lili, 'you do.'

'I won't always be here,' Anna said evenly. Pieter had died so suddenly. She wanted to mend fences with her daughter if only to spare her the bitter, unresolved emotions she had experienced then. She still loved Lili enough to want her not to have to go through that; no, she'd not have wished such pain upon anyone, least of all her only daughter. But Lili had fixed ideas about her parents' marriage.

'Are you happy?' Anna asked timidly.

'Of course not,' was the reply. 'How can I be? Haven't I told you time and again the upbringing you gave me left me so lacking in confidence and self-esteem that I don't expect to ever find what you call happiness.'

Anna knew she would have to reply carefully to this. What she wanted to say was that Lili was being ridiculous, she was a woman in her thirties, her destiny was in her own hands. No one was dealt the hand they thought they deserved in life, you just had to make the best of it. To blame your mother for your misery at Lili's age was just wallowing in self-pity, as far as Anna was concerned. She had been a good enough mother, of that Anna was convinced. She had always given Lili her freedom and respected her independence. What did Lili want? That her mother live her life for her? Only by completely abdicating responsibility for her own life could Lili hold Anna to account. She didn't say any of this aloud. Instead, she took a deep breath and said quietly. 'One thing which you should always remember, and yet one which you always choose to overlook, is that I didn't leave your father. He left me.'

'But then he came back and you wouldn't take him in.'

'Why should I have done so?' Anna was dismayed to see how quickly she was losing her temper, when she had wanted so much to stay calm. 'Have you any idea what it's like to have a man walk out on you like that? The man to whom you promised and devoted your whole life? Do you know what it's like to have a child with a man, and then to have him humiliate you in the worst possible way, in front of all your family and friends?'

When Lili was ten, Pieter had left Anna for his secretary. He was forty, Anna two years younger, and the secretary was nineteen. Anna hadn't suspected a thing. She had thought they were happy together. One evening Pieter didn't come home from work. He rang her later to say that he wouldn't be home that night, that he wouldn't be home again at all, except to collect his belongings. Anna felt she aged ten years that evening. She had never given a moment's thought to getting older, had noticed slight, gradual changes in her skin, her body, as just that, changes, not as a deterioration of which to be frightened. She'd had nothing but contempt for women who at forty thought they should look as they did at twenty. After Lili was born, she was never as shapely as she'd been before, but she didn't care. She was proud of her body. The changes wrought by motherhood made her feel more womanly, not less. But then Pieter walked out on her for a teenager, and Anna felt he might as well have said straight out she was fat, old and ugly. She still knew she had been right in her earlier attitude, but the shock of his betrayal completely destroyed her self-confidence. She rebuilt her life, but she never got over that particular shock.

'It was just a silly little fling, Mother, anybody could see that. I remember at the time, everybody told you it would just blow over. I've never understood why you took it all so seriously, it was just too banal.'

'Banal!' Anna shrieked, jumping up from her seat. 'Don't you realize what you're saying? That's what made it so humiliating for me. Why can't you see that? Are you a woman at all, Lili, that I can't make you see that?'

'But then he wanted to come back and you wouldn't take him.'

'No,' Anna said, 'that isn't true. It wasn't that I wouldn't take him back: I couldn't. He had stayed away too long.'

'Ten months! You call that long!'

'Yes. Yes I do. You don't measure that sort of time by the calendar. You can't quantify pain like that. I spent those months hardening my heart just so I'd be able to go on living, and look after you. It was the only way I had to protect myself. By the time they got bored with each other and she kicked him out, it was too late. I couldn't just forgive and forget and go back to being as we had been before. Maybe you can turn your heart on and off like a tap, but I can't.' She forced herself to be calm, and spoke quietly now. 'My marriage failed because your father left me, not because I refused to forgive him. It was not my fault. I did everything I could to try to protect you, to lessen the hurt, but I had my limits. I think I gave you a good upbringing under the circumstances, but all you do is blame me. It isn't fair. The troubles of your life are not my fault, Lili. Can't you understand that? They are not my fault.'

She was shouting again by that point. Lili walked over to the door and coldly requested that she leave.

That was last time she saw Lili, although Anna had attempted to contact her several times since then. All letters remained unanswered. Once she went to the apartment block where Lili lived. She rang the bell repeatedly, but there was no response, even though there were lights at the window, and Anna knew that her daughter must be there. The block was protected by a complex set of security devices. When Anna rang the bell a light came on, and a closed-circuit television camera was activated. Standing on the doorstep, pleading through the security system, 'Let me in, Lili, please, just for a moment, I must talk to you,' she imagined her daughter standing in a warm hallway, looking at the image of her mother's face on the tiny grey screen, listening to her tearful, pleading voice, but not yielding, making no reply, showing her no mercy.

Once Rita had asked her what she liked most about Donegal, and Anna, remembering that evening, had replied, 'I like the way everyone leaves the key of their house sticking in the front door.'

These thoughts and memories had tormented her tonight as she tossed in bed, longing for sleep to come. She'd been reminded of Lili by Nuala that afternoon, even before the young woman started to pour out her woes under the influence of the clear spirit Anna offered her. Like Lili, Nuala had strikingly beautiful hands. Both wore tinkling bracelets and rings set with precious stones which showed off to advantage their white fingers and perfectly manicured nails. Lili was a bank teller, and Anna had often noticed that women whose jobs involved counting out money tended to be vain about their hands.

Nuala told her something of why she was in Donegal: of her mother's death, of how she had taken it for granted that she'd be there to help her with the baby, and how upset she'd been when it turned out so differently. Anna was shocked at the sudden, violent antipathy she felt for the young woman, founded as it was on nothing other than pure envy for the love there had been between Nuala and her mother. Why was she excluded from such a love? She struggled to hide her feelings: knowing they were unfair was little help, and she was afraid that she would go too far, that she would vent on a bewildered Nuala all the pent-up resentments she felt towards Lili. With supreme effort she kept her counsel, and as a result spent the night drinking whiskey to insulate herself against the pain of her own memories.

9

WHEN CLAIRE ANSWERED THE PHONE one morning and heard Kevin's voice, she assumed he wanted to talk with Nuala. She wasn't at home. It was a strange time for him to call, for they usually rang each other at prearranged times. Nuala would answer the phone when she expected that the call was for her, so it was the first time Claire and Kevin had spoken since Nuala's arrival. 'I think she's out visiting a friend. She goes out most days.'

Claire was keen to cut the conversation at that, and promised to tell Nuala he had rung, but Kevin persisted. 'How's she getting on there?' Gradually it dawned on Claire that Kevin had rung precisely because he guessed Nuala would not be at home. Claire didn't want to talk about Nuala in her absence, and replied vaguely to his questions.

'Oh, it's hard to tell, I think things are going well.'

'Is she happy there?' he asked bluntly.

'Well, she has no reason not to be,' said Claire, nettled. 'Why don't you ask her yourself, Kevin? I told you, she'll be back by tea time, you can talk to her then.'

'Oh. Oh, all right, then.' He sounded disconsolate, and she relented slightly, feeling sorry for him.

'Look, there really isn't much I can tell you. She's

getting lots of fresh air and rest, and I take it that's what she came here for. I just don't feel it's my place to give you a report on her, you ought to talk to her about this yourself. Listen, here's an idea. Why don't you come up to Donegal for the weekend? You can stay here, you'd be very welcome.' But Kevin met this suggestion with little enthusiasm.

He didn't want to tell Claire that he had already suggested to Nuala that he come and visit her, and he'd been hurt by how quickly she rejected that offer. 'I don't think that would be a good idea at all,' she'd said with a decisiveness which surprised him. Brooding on this had prompted him to ring Claire, to try to find out what the situation was, but she appeared not to want to tell him.

'One last thing,' he said, 'does she ever talk about going home?'

'Not really,' said Claire, which she hoped was more gentle than saying 'Never.' Standing in her draughty hallway, she imagined Kevin, miserable in his elegant front room. They continued to talk in a desultory fashion, for she didn't want to hurt him any more by bringing the conversation to an abrupt finish. As they talked, she began to feel glad that he hadn't accepted her offer to come and stay, for she realized how nervous it would have made her. It was years since she'd seen him. Even hearing his voice the first time he had called up to ask if Nuala could stay had unsettled her more than she cared to admit. He sounded exactly the same as ever, but she knew that they had changed over the years, both of them, and not just in looks. She didn't know how she would react to the memories meeting Kevin would draw up, and was relieved that such a meeting now was unlikely.

Two days later, Claire rang Kevin. It was eight o'clock in the morning. His voice was drowsy as he answered the phone. Nuala had remarked once that they were late risers, because of working every night in the restaurant.

'Hi, Kevin, it's me. Stay calm now, don't worry.' Even as she spoke, she knew he was in a panic, leaping from the bed, fully awake.

'Claire, it's about Nuala, I know, what's wrong, tell me quickly, what's happened?'

'It's nothing Kevin: well, I mean I hope it's nothing serious. It's just that – well, Nuala went out yesterday afternoon and she . . . she still hasn't come back.'

Claire paused to give Kevin a moment to take this in. 'I thought long and hard before I rang you, because it could all be completely innocent.' She regretted these words as soon as she had spoken them: they so clearly cast Nuala in a guilty light. 'I don't want you to worry, Kevin. The crime rate round here is zero, so the chances of her having been abducted are a million to one.'

'Couldn't she have fallen off a cliff, or broken her leg while out walking?'

'I . . . I . . . don't think so. She wasn't headed that way when she left the house.' This was turning out to be even worse than she had thought it would be. She had dreaded all night making this phone call. She couldn't bring herself to give Kevin a full picture of the situation.

After lunch, the previous day, Nuala had gone out for a walk. Claire, working in the studio, heard her leave the house. She looked out of the window and saw Nuala walk to the bottom of the lane, and then turn right, away from the cliffs and the sea. Claire supposed she was on her way to visit Anna, and these visits could be lengthy.

Occasionally they went into town together in Anna's car, or sometimes she stayed there for meals. As Nuala usually did the cooking in Claire's house, she always made a point of telling her if she was going to be out. So Claire, busy with her work, didn't think much about Nuala's absence.

Dinner time came, and Nuala had still not returned. Claire started to prepare a meal, thinking she would arrive before it was ready, but still there was no sign of her. Claire put Nuala's dinner in the oven to keep warm, and sat down to eat her own meal. No, there was nothing else for it. She swore loudly, put a bowl over her dinner to keep it warm, and rang Anna.

It relieved Claire to some extent that Anna was not troubled by the situation which Claire presented to her. Yes, Nuala had called with her that afternoon. She had been in good spirits, 'perhaps a little bit bored', Anna said. ('Bored!' thought Claire. 'I'll give her bored when I get my hands on her!') She had stayed for an hour or so, and when she left, she said that she was going to go up to Rita's shop to buy some chocolate before going home.

'Right, I'd best ring Rita, then,' Claire said.

Anna was bemused. 'Don't you think you're over-reacting somewhat?' she asked, but Claire was indignant at this. 'Ring Rita, then,' Anna said, 'if it'll make you feel better.'

Rita told her that Nuala had been in the shop at just the time Anna had mentioned. There had been another woman there too, a Miss Byrne, did Claire know her? She had said something about driving into town, and Rita had seen Nuala pay attention when she said this. She left the shop before Miss Byrne, but Rita noticed that

Nuala had waited outside and spoke to the other woman when she came out. For the first time ever, Claire was glad that Rita was so tremendously curious about other people.

'Do you think she went into town with Miss Byrne?'

'I think that more than probable,' Rita said. Miss Byrne had been going to stay with her sister there who wasn't well. After she had said goodbye to Rita, Claire tried to ring Miss Byrne, but, as she had expected, there was no reply. So, Claire deduced, Nuala had gone into town, probably on a sudden whim, thinking she could spend an hour or two there and then get a lift back with someone, not realizing that the cars that went out as far as where Claire lived were few enough during the day, but there were none at all after a certain time in the evening. So Nuala would be stuck in town.

There were two flaws to this theory. The first was that the logical succession to this would be that Nuala would phone to explain what had happened, and either tell Claire she would stay the night there, or ask that Claire come and fetch her. But she didn't phone. The other flaw was that since her arrival, she had gone to town several times. Sometimes she went with Anna, sometimes she borrowed Claire's car and went by herself to do shopping, or simply to have a change of scene. She'd always told Claire what she'd done when she got back, she wasn't at all secretive about these visits: not that there was much there you could do that would merit conceal-ment, Claire thought.

'Maybe she just decided all of a sudden,' Anna said that night when Claire phoned her again. 'Maybe when she heard that Miss Byrne was going to town, she decided to go too. I still think there's no need to worry. You know, Claire,' Anna went on, 'Nuala is a grown woman, a married woman, she is free to go where she pleases. I told you I thought she was bored this afternoon. Perhaps she wanted a little adventure.'

'Well, she's picked a bloody odd place to have it,' said Claire. Anna was evidently less well integrated than Claire had imagined, if she hadn't grasped this basic point about rural Ireland: that it lacked the anonymity essential for 'little adventures'.

'I'm talking about something completely innocent,' Anna persisted, who thought Claire was less worldly and sophisticated than she woud have given her credit for. 'Nuala probably just wanted to be alone for a night, with no one knowing where she is, nor who she is.' Anna urged Claire to put it out of her mind. 'Get a good night's sleep and I tell you, she'll be home before lunch time tomorrow.'

It was beyond Claire's power to sleep well that night, even though she reasoned with herself that Nuala was, as Anna had pointed out, a grown woman. Simply because Nuala was staying in her house didn't make Claire responsible for her every move. But logic could not ease the thought that if Nuala did not turn up, Kevin would have to be told. She dreaded ringing him. Against the agonies of wondering what she would say to Kevin, she consoled herself by imagining what she would say to Nuala – no, what she would *do* to her – when she did finally reappear.

She got out of bed at six, and put off ringing Kevin until eight. She was afraid that if she waited until mid-morning he would have left the house, and she would have been unable to track him down. He wanted to leave for Donegal at once, but she dismissed this, and told him she would call again in a couple of hours. Just before ten o'clock, Kevin rang her. Claire had no news for him. He told her he was setting out immediately, and this time she didn't argue. He promised to stop every hour or so en route, to call her and see if there was any news. She gave up the idea of any serious work, and began to sort out materials in the studio simply to give her something with which to occupy herself.

It was just after eleven o'clock when she heard the front door being opened. Like most people locally, Claire left the key in her door when she was inside. She left the studio, and as she came downstairs she could see that Nuala was already in the hall, draping her damp raincoat over the bannisters. 'Terrible weather,' she remarked to Claire as she went up the hall and into the kitchen. Claire followed her, silently, staring at her with something between fascination and fury.

'Like some tea?' Nuala said, taking the kettle over to the sink to fill it. There was a long, sinister pause.

'No, thanks, I've just had a cup,' Claire eventually replied. The words in themselves were innocuous, but from the tone in which they were spoken, Nuala knew she was in deep trouble. She wondered how Claire was capable of putting such venom and threat into such a harmless phrase. Nuala sighed theatrically, put the kettle down and turned to Claire.

If Claire's mental rehearsals for her conversation with Kevin had been of no help, the same was not true of her plans to confront Nuala. There was a little resistance at first, but it didn't really take long to wear her down.

Nuala confessed to what Anna had predicted would be the scenario. Nuala had felt very restless the day before. She'd gone to buy chocolate and heard a woman in the shop say she was going into town. On impulse, Nuala asked to go with her. She hadn't thought through what she would do there or how she would get back. After a while, she'd decided to stay the night, so she found a bed and breakfast place.

'It was really horrible,' she said, as though this somehow exonerated her. 'You should have seen the room, it had an orange candlewick bedspread.'

'Why didn't you ring me?'

'I tried,' Nuala said. She and Claire both knew that this was a lie. 'I did try, but I couldn't get through.' Claire wondered if it was worth the energy to argue with her about this, and decided it wasn't. She still had a card to play.

Nuala felt pleased at getting away with such a lie. She didn't intend to tell Claire everything about her trip to town. She didn't tell her how she'd gone into the local chipper for her evening meal, and had eaten cod and chips off a formica table, while some children fed coins into a loud, flickering fruit machine. She'd looked at the clotted sauce bottles before her, and wondered what was it about her life, what choices had she made (or failed to make) that she had ended up getting her thrills by stealing ashtrays and sneaking off to spend the night alone in a dreary B&B, eating fish and chips doused in malt vinegar? She'd thought of Kevin. At that exact moment he would be in the restaurant, overseeing the serving of monkfish in dill sauce. What would Kevin think if he could see her? It wouldn't be worse to him than infidelity, but certainly a lot harder to understand. He would be able to see the point of her going with another man, even if it upset him, but her sitting in a chipper with a one and one and a tin of cherryade would be beyond his comprehension. But then of course, Nuala herself didn't understand it.

'So that's all there was to it,' she said to Claire, with as much innocence as she could muster. 'It was nice too, for me just to have a little time completely by myself.'

'But didn't you ever think how worried I would be? Let alone Kevin . . .'

'Kevin? You didn't tell Kevin! Oh Claire! Oh God!'

Claire felt only slightly guilty about the stab of delight she felt on seeing Nuala's utter dismay. 'Of course I told Kevin,' she said suavely. 'How was I to know where you were? You could have fallen off a cliff. What was I to do? Wait three days until you were washed up on the strand and ring him then?' Nuala and Claire both knew these were rhetorical questions. 'I waited all night and when you still hadn't shown up this morning, I phoned him.' Claire paused, (cruelly, she knew,) for maximum effect, and then added lightly, 'He's on his way here now.'

Nuala put her head in her hands and moaned. Right on cue, the telephone rang. Even Claire felt sorry for Nuala at that point. 'Don't worry,' she said, 'I'll deal with it.' She went into the hall and picked up the receiver. Nuala stood in the kitchen doorway, looking at her nervously.

'Hi, Kevin,' Claire said. 'Good news. Nuala's back. Yes, she's fine, as I said, it was nothing to get seriously worked up about.' She'd been looking at Nuala until that moment, but dropped her gaze, and half turned aside, speaking more softly. 'Oh, I don't remember, she said something about missing a bus or something, I haven't really asked her yet.' Claire listened for a moment, then said, 'That would be difficult right now.' She turned round and looked at Nuala again. 'She's in the bath.' Claire listened again, and laughed. 'No, I can't, believe it or not I still have one of those phones that are fixed in one place, you have to come to it.' She made some dismissive remarks: Kevin was evidently thanking her and apologizing for the worry.

'Whatever you think,' she said in conclusion, looking again at Nuala. 'As you're on the road, if you want to come here, feel free . . .'

Claire said goodbye and hung up. 'Kevin's on his way,' she said.

10

WHEN KEVIN WAS GROWING UP, his mother had given him some advice. 'If ever you think of marrying a girl, take a long hard look at her mother first.' It was the only solid, explicit warning she had ever given him, (the only one he could remember, anyway). Naturally, he paid no heed to this, except after he was married, when, in the company of either Nuala or her mother, he would often find himself turning the idea over in his mind. It was too late by then. Sometimes he was afraid that Nuala would know what he was thinking. 'Penny for your thoughts, Kevin,' she would say sharply, and he would reply, 'Oh nothing – nothing at all. I just wondered . . .' and then he would garble out the first thing he could think of to distract her. Sometimes she frightened him. He didn't understand her.

But driving out of Dublin that morning when she was missing, he asked himself if, in all honesty, he regretted marrying her, and he realized that he didn't. If he had his life to live over, he would have married Nuala again, if only out of a sense of inevitability. To think in this way at all was unusual for him. He thought it was foolish to spend too much time analysing your life and circumstances. It could do little good, as far as Kevin was concerned, and perhaps do harm, arousing discontentment and desires about which nothing could be done. Kevin and Nuala: of course they were married, of course they were together, that was the way it always was. In his heart, Kevin was contemptuous of people who expected marriage – indeed, who expected anything – to make them happy. He couldn't understand people who expected their lives to be a contented, upward curve of social and economic achievement, rounded out by personal happiness. What was wrong with them? Didn't they open their eyes and look around? Surely then they would see that such things only happened in movies and magazines. Sometimes he used to argue with Nuala about this, but when he said that people nowadays expected too much from life, she would always say, 'Oh, don't be such an old fogey. The real problem was that in the past, people didn't expect enough.'

He took being married completely for granted, and up until now, he hadn't seen anything wrong with this, (although he knew better than to say so out loud, especially to Nuala). It had always seemed inevitable that he would be married, and there had never seemed any possibility that it would be to anyone other than Nuala. The thought of her no longer being in his life struck him as absurd, rather than painful. He couldn't remember meeting her. She'd been his sister's best friend at school, and had been in and out of the house from about the age of twelve. She'd always been piggish about sweets: his earliest memory of her concerned the phenomenal quantity of chocolates she put away one evening in their house. That hadn't changed over the years, whatever else had. Later on, she came to the house just to see him, not to visit his sister. She'd been his first real girlfriend, and neither of their mothers had been happy about it. They said they thought it was too serious, they were afraid they'd get married as soon as they left school, that they'd distract each other from their studies, and so on. The real reasons were that neither mother liked her child's choice: Nuala's mother thought Kevin was feckless because he was planning to go to art school, because he wasn't as respectable as she would have wanted him to be. Kevin's mother frankly told him she thought Nuala was 'a minx'. 'It's not just that she always has to get her own way: it's the way she manages to make it look like chance or other people's doing that I don't like,' she said, an observation so astute that Kevin was taken aback when his mother said it to him. He'd lost his virginity to Nuala earlier that month: it had all been Nuala's idea, but without anything in particular being said, she had been able to make it look like it was all his doing, and she had yielded to him, rather than the other way round. Like the prodigious chocolate consumption, it was a trick she could still turn, years later.

Both sets of parents had been pleased when they went to college and happier still when the weekend visits cooled off and they gradually lost contact with each other and started seeing other people. They hadn't even liked each other at that period, on the rare occasions when they met. She thought what he was doing was a childish waste of time. He loathed the clothes she now wore: stiff suits with shoulder pads and fake pearls, floppy bows at the neck of her blouses, the uniform of the business women whose ranks she wanted to join. Kevin thought it looked sterile. He didn't think he could have anything in common with someone who looked like that.

And yet as soon as they graduated they were together again within weeks. Before much more time had passed, they were planning their wedding, their house, their future life together. Kevin would never have claimed that he had drifted into marriage. 'Drift' was far too mild a word for the speed and velocity with which it happened. And it had never troubled him, never struck him as anything other than logical that it should be so.

Only now, when there was so clearly something wrong in his marriage did he stop to consider it carefully, to think what it might be. He hadn't kept Nuala down, he was sure of that. If anything, he had deferred to her, knowing her to be stronger and shrewder than he. Kevin didn't mind admitting that all their success with the restaurant had been due to Nuala.

They had both been doing reasonably well in the first years after they married. Nuala had been working with an insurance company in the city centre, Kevin had had a job in a commercial gallery. He would probably have been content to plod along in that way for years, but for a casual remark. They had gone out to dinner in a restaurant one night, and at the end of the meal, like countless other people before him, he'd said over the coffee and mints, 'Wouldn't it be lovely if we had our own restaurant?' Afterwards, he couldn't remember Nuala making any significant reply to this. It was a dream he had had for a long time, and he was disconcerted when Nuala came to him a week later, all briskness, with the facts and figures on a sheet of paper, announcing that having their own restaurant might well be a viable possibility. She had been to talk to their bank manager, had looked around at possible properties, had spoken to her father about a loan (Kevin wasn't at all happy about that,) and was still engaged in looking at the restaurants already in operation in Dublin to see what gap there was in the market. When Nuala spoke of it, it all sounded so real that it frightened him. 'But what if it fails?' he kept saying nervously.

'It won't fail because by the time I've finished doing my investigations I'll know whether or not it's a runner, and if it isn't, then we won't do it.'

'Lots of restaurants fold,' Kevin murmured.

'Yes, of course they do, and do you know why? Because they're run by people who know a lot about food, but don't realize that they're running a business. But I know how to run a business. See if I don't!'

It was no empty boast. Kevin had watched anxiously as she carefully worked out all the financial aspects of the project before making a final decision. It brought out, or rather, it exposed to him, a side of Nuala that he hadn't been aware of up until then. He wasn't always sure that he liked it. Later, when staff they hired turned out to be unsatisfactory, Nuala fired them without a qualm. She'd insisted that it be an Irish restaurant: they had argued a bit about that, but of course he had given in at last, and of course she had been right. She left the hiring of a chef and the choice of décor to Kevin. She'd been right in everything. The restaurant quickly established a good reputation, and was now a popular and long-established feature of the Dublin social scene.

Nominally it was a partnership, but it was due to Nuala's confidence and ability that it existed at all. Kevin had learnt so much from her that he was now able to manage the place well in her absence, but he would never forget that it was all due to Nuala. He could never have done it on his own, and he loved it, loved the atmosphere of the place, the social status and the comfortable lifestyle it gave them. Nuala's attitude was strange, though, and that troubled him. She wasn't even very interested in food, she was cynical about the enterprise, he often thought, and would get cross when he complained about this. But she'd been like that right from the start, he didn't understand what was troubling her so much now. Because he was never in the habit of reasoning out situations, particularly situations of emotional complexity, he didn't know what to make of the present circumstances. He couldn't bear to think that something had happened to Nuala. The thought of life without her frightened him. He started to look out anxiously for a phone box.

Resentment and relief struggled to get the upper hand when Claire told him that Nuala had turned up safe and well. He decided to press on and go to Donegal: he had to talk to Nuala about all this immediately. To turn round and go straight back to Dublin would be cowardly. As he drove on, he considered that he would also see Claire. That would be a mixed pleasure. It would be odd to see Nuala and Claire together, he considered them as each belonging to such separate phases of his life that it didn't seem possible that they could both be there simultaneously. He wondered, not for the first time, if it had really been such a good idea for Nuala to stay in Claire's house. How much was he to blame in this? Maybe he had handled it in the worst possible way in sending her away. Had he just panicked, and thought about what would happen to the business if news of Nuala's stealing things got about? But there had to be more to it than that. What had made her steal in the first place?

Was it the baby? Had he, perhaps without even being aware of it, pressurized her into having a baby she didn't want? No, he was sure that it was not so (although he had to admit that he viewed the child with the same sense of inevitability that he saw in his marriage). No, Nuala had wanted the child, she'd seemed contented with the idea perhaps more before the baby was born than after its birth. But that wasn't too surprising: Nuala always enjoyed looking forward to things more than the thing itself. 'How come nothing is ever as good as you think it's going to be?' she said, peevishly, on more occasions than he cared to remember. But he always thought it was clear what Nuala was after, even if she was able to persuade you that it was your idea and wish rather than hers. He couldn't help feeling that she ought to be happy, but he knew that thinking so did nothing to alleviate the fact that she was clearly miserable.

Around noon, he pulled the car over to the side of the road and took out his lunch. In spite of the circumstances in which he had left the house, he hadn't neglected to take some food with him: french bread, some cold beef, a wedge of Roquefort cheese, fruit, bottled water. He remembered with horror some of the things he'd been offered in hotels and restaurants in rural Ireland on his rare forays out of the city. When Kevin left Dublin, he was only really happy if he was on his way to the airport. He associated long drives across the country with his childhood, when they went to visit his granny in

Tipperary. He'd never liked those visits. Even as a child he had been picky about his food; and even by the standards of the time and place, his granny had been an atrocious cook. He could still remember her gristly stew, and loaves of soda bread, baked to the consistency of a breeze block. As he ate the Roquefort, he remembered how she'd once found an old piece of Cheddar which had been forgotten at the back of the larder for weeks, and was covered with a hairy blue mould when she took it out. She'd set it on the kitchen table and said with amazement, 'Now if you were to give that to a Frenchman, he'd probably think it was the nicest thing that ever he ate.'

It had been raining when he left the city, and now, as he sat in the parked car, rain lashed against the windscreen. He switched on the ignition, and briefly turned on the wipers. The Bog of Allen appeared before him, as abruptly and vividly as if he'd switched on a television set: rich brown earth, flat under a complicated sky full of heavy grey clouds. Christ, what a dump! Kevin thought he would rather be bricked up behind a wall than live in such a desolate spot. And yet he had sent Nuala to a place like this, a place where there was nothing. How could she be expected to survive without dress shops and department stores, without a bit of activity going on around her? Maybe she was angry with him, and wanted to give him a fright by doing a bunk for the night. He'd have certainly resented it if he'd been packed off from the city for the summer like that. He switched off the wipers, and let the falling rain obliterate the gloomy scene before him.

But Nuala was happy in Donegal. She didn't want to

come home. It hurt him deeply to think this. Did she dislike him so much? What had he ever done to her to make her feel so hostile to him? He looked at the dashboard, the crumpled paper containing bread and meat on the seat beside him. He listened to the rain, and suddenly he thought: I want to stay here. He didn't want to drive on to Donegal, to face Nuala or Claire or anybody, he just wanted to stay there quietly for as long as possible, all day, until night fell, and perhaps on through the night, because life was so baffling, so bloody *sad* that he just wanted to withdraw from it and be left in peace.

Was that what she felt too?

With deep reluctance he put away the remains of his lunch, and continued on his way.

11

THE CHIP SHOP where Nuala went the night she stayed away wasn't the only place locally where you could get a meal. There had been a degree of wilful perversity in her choosing to go there, rather than to some of the restaurants and hotels which had appeared as a result of the tourist trade. Claire suggested two possibilities: a hotel in town which she said did decent meals, and a restaurant called The Silver Salmon, which was patronized not only by tourists, but also the local fishermen and their families, when the catch had been good and they were in funds. They chose to go to the latter.

Kevin looked ironically at his plate, piled high with steak in a wine sauce, carrots, peas, and a mountain of chips. 'Obviously nouvelle cuisine hasn't got as far as Donegal,' he said.

'No, and I'll tell you why, Kevin. It's because the people here have more sense than to pay fifteen quid for a piece of meat the size of a stamp, with one mushroom sitting on top of it. They work too hard for their money here to waste it on nonsense like that.' Food was the only thing Kevin and Nuala had rows about, sometimes quite serious ones. When they came home from a meal where style had been more important than substance, Nuala would go straight to the fridge and get herself a hunk of bread and cheese, grumbling loudly. 'What sort of idiots are we to pay money like that and end up coming home as hungry as we were when we left the house?' Kevin used to wither with shame when she came out with things like that in front of his friends. He was afraid too, that people would get to know what she thought and that it would reflect badly on the restaurant.

She let her cynicism about the business show much more than was necessary, he often told her, as she mocked the customers behind their backs. 'They deserve it,' she insisted. 'People just follow fashion, Kevin. They don't know how to think for themselves.' Sometimes she turned her invective on Kevin himself. 'Who do you think you're fooling, with your wild-nettle sauces and your wilted greens! You grew up on spuds, peas and chops, the same as everybody else.' He'd tell her she was greedy and unsophisticated, but he knew she was every bit as choosy as he, and that a lot of it was just talk, or done to annoy him. But knowing this often didn't help. 'When all's said and done, it's just a bit of dinner, isn't it?' was a remark she could always rely on to infuriate him.

But tonight Nuala obviously regretted her remark about nouvelle cuisine as soon as she had said it. 'Eat what you can, if there's too much there for you,' she said quietly, picking up her knife and fork.

All told, things weren't going anything like as badly as Nuala had feared they would. Claire had come through with far more help and kindness than she had expected, and Nuala thought of her with gratitude. She suggested sensibly that Nuala should be out of the house when

97

Kevin arrived, and rang Anna to ask if Nuala could wait there. So it had been from Anna's window that she saw Kevin's car drive past, and she waited there for over half an hour before setting out to walk slowly, so very slowly back to Claire's house. 'Time to face the music,' she said ruefully to Anna, pretending to a levity she certainly didn't feel, and which didn't convince Anna for a moment.

She wondered what Claire had said to Kevin, or what had passed between them before she arrived to make the atmosphere so relaxed and even cheerful. She realized now how nervous she'd been going into the room, afraid that Kevin would be cold and hostile, even that he would be angry and start to shout at her in front of Claire (but that had been a foolish notion: that wasn't Kevin's style at all). Without saying anything, he came straight over to her, and put his arms around her, hugged her tightly and kissed her. Nuala was enormously relieved. Claire stayed in the room with them for another three quarters of an hour or so: Nuala had feared that she would bolt off on some pretext as soon as Nuala arrived, leaving them alone together immediately. They had drunk tea and chatted in what was a remarkably relaxed and amiable fashion, given the circumstances.

Still, she knew that the hour of reckoning was to come sooner or later, and now, in the restaurant, she was afraid that at any moment Kevin would put down his knife and fork and begin to demand serious answers. She tried to evade this with chatter about anything she could think of: harmless anecdotes about Anna and Claire, and the life she had been leading since coming to Donegal. Kevin let her talk. She didn't like the way he was looking at her, but was willing to admit that perhaps she was just reading her own guilt into his face. Any other time she would have confronted him with it: 'Penny for your thoughts, Kevin. What are you looking so serious about?' but tonight she'd have given him anything for him to keep his thoughts strictly to himself.

She was reading him wrongly. Kevin's actual mood, (as Nuala might have guessed, had she thought about it coolly) was one of weariness and disorientation. At exactly this time the night before, he had been standing in his own restaurant in Monkstown. The last place on earth he expected to be twenty-four hours later was sitting opposite Nuala in The Silver Salmon. He'd had to make hurried arrangements at work and find someone to mind the baby, then there had been the worry of wondering what had happened to Nuala, was it his fault that this had happened? And on top of all that, there was sheer weariness, after the long drive across the country. He was glad just to be here and to find Nuala well. The last thing he planned to do tonight was to stir up trouble, or to 'have it out' with Nuala, as she herself would have expressed it.

It had been strange for him to see Claire again. Only now could he admit how nervous he'd been about that. Once he knew Nuala was safe, for the remainder of the journey he'd been at least as preoccupied about seeing Claire as he had about seeing his wife. He had an image of Claire in his mind from over ten years ago, and he knew that when he met her again he would have to readjust that image. He didn't want to see Claire looking older, more to the point, he didn't want to see how she would react to an older version of him. And Claire had never been – how could he put it? – a *comfortable* person. She'd had a way of looking at you sideways that he had always found upsetting, and he had discovered this afternoon that she could still do it. She had changed much less than he expected. But he'd remembered, too, all the reasons why he had liked her so much in the past. He'd found himself thinking 'What if?' and Claire looking at him sideways, wordlessly telling him to forget it. It had been a relief when Nuala came timidly into the room.

After the waitress cleared away their plates he said, 'I don't want to talk about why you went away – not tonight, in any case. There'll be time for that when we get back to Dublin.'

'Oh, I don't have to go back just yet, do I?'

'Of course you do,' he said coldly, hurt at her reluctance to come home. 'It's too much of a responsibility to ask Claire to keep you here after what happened yesterday. She was more worried than you perhaps realize, but the main thing is that she thinks if you're behaving like that, then it's clear you're not happy here, so there's little point in your staying on.'

'But I am happy! I am! I like it here. I'm not ready to go home yet.'

'Well, it isn't up to me, is it? You'll have to talk to Claire about it. It's her house, and she's been exceptionally kind in having you to stay for so long already. But she is worried about the consequences of your being there.'

'Nothing like yesterday will happen again, I promise it won't.'

'I've already told you, Nuala, it isn't up to me.' Kevin

said. 'If you have an promises to make, make them to Claire. The matter is out of my hands. It's up to her whether or not she wants to let you go on staying with her.' She wasn't even trying to hide how eager she was to remain away from home. He called the waitress back, and ordered a black coffee and no dessert.

'I think the least you could do would be agree to spend a little time with me. I want you to come down to Sligo with me for a night or two.' He delivered this firmly. Nuala knew just how far she could push him. 'That would be lovely. I like Sligo.' Their marriage was, to a large extent, a complicated system of bargain and compromise, the rules of which Nuala understood implicitly, even if she didn't always abide by them. She'd known he wouldn't like this part of Donegal. No, they could do worse than go to some gentrified little hotel in Sligo for a night or two, she'd think of how she was going to explain herself on the drive there. She called over the waitress, and asked for some dessert.

A glass-fronted trolley was wheeled to their table, and the waitress listed off the names of the confections it contained: chocolate mousse, pineapple gâteau, pavlova, fruit salad, crème caramel. Nuala chose pavlova. Was she doing this deliberately to annoy him, he wondered, as a huge helping of meringue was placed before her. The plate was scarcely big enough to hold it. There were few things Kevin thought more vulgar than large, inelegant desserts.

'Yum yum!' said Nuala, taking up her spoon. The waitress removed the trolley to the far side of the room. It was a quiet night, for a Friday in July, but the waitresses were glad enough of that. When things were slack, they would gossip in the kitchen and speculate about the customers. They all did it, but the girl who served Nuala and Kevin that evening had practically raised it to an art form. Her speciality was to make outrageous speculations about the people at the tables the other waitresses were on, and she'd pass on these wild conjectures between courses, so then the others would have trouble keeping a straight face when they went back for the dessert orders.

They'd have died of embarrassment if they could have heard some of the things she said about them: not that she had any sympathy with them. That was the thing she really didn't like about working as a waitress: you got to see the worst side of people. It would put you off humanity: certainly put you off getting married. Sometimes she felt sorry for people, but generally she thought it was their own fault. She looked across at the couple she had just finished serving, wishing the woman would finish her bloody pavlova and pay and go so that she could finish up and go home herself. They were definitely a married couple: she prided herself on being able to tell the ones that were really married, the ones that weren't, and the ones who were pretending, who were there with people they shouldn't have been with. This pair were no ad for wedded bliss, that was for sure. He looked nice: well, he would have looked nicer if he hadn't had a face on him as long as a late breakfast. Could you blame him, married to her? You could tell just looking at her she was spoiled rotten, used to getting her own way all the time, and still not contented. What did people want out of life, anyway? They obviously had lots of money, for she had such beautiful clothes. You could tell a good thing by the colour as much as the cut, and that peachy shade of her linen jacket didn't come cheap.

The waitress narrowed her eyes and stared even harder at them. Sometimes she just invented crazy stories to make the other girls laugh, but she could also work out how things really were just by looking at people. This pair had been married not a long time, but not so recently either. Maybe seven or eight years at a guess. Long enough to feel really married, to have got to the point where security stopped being a relief and started to be a pain in the neck. It wasn't that she was taking it for granted, it was different. Her sister was married, so she'd seen this sort of thing before. Nobody wanted to have a marriage that was shaky, ready to fall apart at any minute, but if it was too copperfastened, well, after a certain time you'd want to put it to the test, to sort of push against it, even kick against it, to see how far you would have to go before something gave. And she'd have bet her week's wage that that was what was happening here, that this spoiled brat was running rings around her husband, rocking the boat just for the sake of it. But if push came to shove, she'd be the first to cry off: if she pushed him so far that he said, 'It's over, let's go our separate ways,' you could be sure she wouldn't like it. The tears there would be then, the fuss she'd make. No, she didn't understand life. She knew how it operated, but she didn't understand it. Did anyone, though?

Kevin and Nuala had finished their meal, and signalled to the waitress to bring them their bill. After they'd gone, she moved to clear the table. They'd left her the biggest tip she'd had all season. She wondered if this was to make up for the fact that they'd taken the pepper pot with them. No, she'd never understand what went on in people's heads, not if she lived to be a hundred.

'MAMMY, WHY IS BLACK BLACK?'

'Because it isn't white.'

'But why?'

'Justice, child, give over with your questions!'

But Claire didn't give over. Throughout her childhood she persistently asked such questions, not to be difficult or contrary, but because she genuinely wanted answers. The subject of colour was important to her even then. Her mother gave her short shrift especially when she demanded to know the colour of people's souls. Her father took it all more patiently. Claire remembered how he would listen to her with an air of great seriousness, his lips pursed, as he tried not to smile at some of the things she said.

'Daddy, why have some birds got blue eggs and some speckledy eggs? How many colours are there in the whole world? Is there a word for the colour a shadow is? Why is grass green? Is white really a colour?'

Her parents both agreed that she would keep a nation going.

She liked the words for the colours: yellow, green, red. Then she learnt new words. Turquoise, vermilion, aquamarine. Ochre, crimson, puce. This love of colour did not diminish as she grew up. The questions never ended, they became more complex, the only difference was that she stopped going to her father for answers to them. She was sitting in the studio reading Frida Kahlo's notes on colour.

BROWN: colour of *mole*, of the leaf that goes. Earth.
YELLOW: madness, sickness, fear. Part of the sun and of joy.
COBALT BLUE: electricity and purity. Love.
BLACK: nothing is black, really *nothing*.

'Daddy,' she'd said when she was eight, 'why do people keep saying the sky is blue, when it almost never is?' He'd laughed aloud at that.

Claire remembered this, turned the page of her book and savoured the silence not just of the studio, but of the whole house. It made her happy to know that she was alone. She somewhat regretted now that she had told Kevin that Nuala could come back on Sunday night to stay until the end of August as had been originally agreed. She had stipulated though that the situation would be – how had she put it? – 'constantly under review', yes, that was it.

She'd discussed this with Kevin in a whispered conversation over breakfast that morning, while Nuala was still upstairs, preparing to leave with Kevin for Sligo. Claire didn't like having to speak so quietly in her own house; it didn't seem right, but she was anxious that Nuala should not hear what she was saying. Claire had lain awake for a long time the night before wondering just what she should say about Nuala staying on. In one way, she just wanted to see the back of her, but she also felt an inexplicable pity for both Kevin and Nuala, and found she couldn't bring herself to be hard on them. But there had to be strict conditions. Looking over at the door, anxious that Nuala would come in at any moment, Claire leaned across the table and said quietly, 'She can come back if she wants. I made a promise, and I don't like to go back on it.' As Kevin started to murmur his thanks, she added hurriedly, 'But you must promise me this. Nuala mustn't know that she can come back until late on Sunday. If she asks, just tell her I haven't made my mind up yet. However, I can tell you now that when you phone me on Sunday afternoon, I'll say yes. It'll be best that way.' Kevin looked puzzled, but he nodded and thanked her.

Claire cut another slice of bread, pleased that they had discussed the subject and that she had made her views known. She simply didn't want Nuala to take her hospitality for granted. 'Keep her guessing until the last minute, that'll teach her,' she thought. 'And can you make one thing clear to her: any more fun and games like the other night, any more disappearing acts and you won't have to come and fetch her, because I won't wait long enough for you to get here. She'll be on the first bus out of town.' Kevin nodded miserably, and suddenly she felt sorry for him again. She offered him more tea, but he shook his head.

'Kevin, while you're away, think hard about Nuala's being here, about whether or not this is the right thing to do,' she urged him. 'Sometimes I'm not at all sure that Donegal is the best place for Nuala right now. Talk to her about it.'

'I'll try to,' he said.

The kitchen door opened at that point, and Nuala came in. Claire saw them off a few moments later, telling them she hoped they would have a great weekend, trying to keep the irony out of her voice. The emptiness of the house after they'd gone was as novel as it was delightful.

No, the sky wasn't blue and the sea wasn't blue either, and often the grass wasn't green. What colour was ice? Water? The sun? This morning it was colourless, a circle of pure light in a white sky. 'Daddy, do you think white is as frightening as black? I do.'

This morning, she wished she had enough money to buy the house where she was living. Up until now, she had had no interest in buying property: still didn't, if she thought it through. Buying would be a declaration of how committed she was to staying in Donegal, rather than a desire to settle down and build a little domestic empire around herself. When Claire moved in, there'd been a small pane of glass broken in the back door. She'd nailed a board over it, and three years later, she still hadn't got round to having the window mended. But even if she bought the house, it didn't necessarily mean that she would then fix it, or that she would do something about the kitchen cupboard that had to be kicked before it would open, or any of the other malfunctioning fixtures and fittings. No, she'd never wanted a house, never even wanted to own things. Once they began to accumulate to any serious degree they made her feel nervous so that she had to get rid of them. Maybe it would be the same if she bought the house, she would immediately feel restless and trapped.

Anyway, it was all hypothetical: she wouldn't buy it because she didn't have enough money. Maybe it was just as well.

From things Kevin had said, she realized he thought she already owned the house. She didn't say anything to disabuse him of the notion. Kevin would have found it incredible that someone could get to Claire's stage in life and not have bought a house, even if it was only a small, draughty, isolated one.

She thought of Giacometti, shocked out of domesticity for ever by an early confrontation with death. It began with a chance, brief meeting on a train with an elderly Dutchman. Later he attempted to, and, amazingly, succeeded in tracing Giacometti through a classified advertisement in a newspaper. They planned a journey together to Venice, but had scarcely set out when the elder man fell ill and died. Giacometti was twenty. The horror he felt on seeing the transition from being to nothingness would never leave him. In the face of certain annihilation, the clutter of domesticity was, to him, a monstrous lie. Why pretend life is anything other than transitory? Why pretend you are anything other than utterly alone in your existence?

Oh, she knew the answer to that all right: because the lies were necessary, because to face the truth was just too damn hard. Because you need Giacometti's courage to bear that sort of knowledge with the integrity he had shown, and the courage is much rarer than the knowledge. What Giacometti learned when his travelling companion died was not such a secret. Claire found it out the night Alice died, and Alice herself had known it all along. She remembered the moon, full over the cold,

109

still peaks, remembered the following morning when she awoke to a strange combination of sorrow and elation. Everything she saw that day was charged with fragility and tenderness: the faces of strangers in the streets, the white mountain houses, the cats that slept on their steps, the pale cattle that were driven through the streets of the village at dusk . . .

It had been strange and sad to see Kevin again. Her first impression was that he looked older than she had expected. He was only in his early thirties, but could easily have passed for ten years more than that. What had ravaged him? Nothing, she discovered with surprise when she looked at him more closely. He was glazed with money, that was the problem. The elegant well-cut clothes, the gold watch, the good accessories all conspired to put years on him. Physically, he was in good shape. It was his mind that had grown old. Her mother would have said that he looked 'highly respectable'. She'd have been right.

Looking at him, Claire wondered not why he had given up painting, but why he had ever concerned himself with it at all. Alice had always had her doubts about him. 'When Kevin is thirty,' she used to say, 'he'll have completely turned himself inside out.' Claire hadn't known then what she meant. She knew now. When he was actually sitting there before her, she found it hard to remember him as he was when she'd known him at art school. They'd had a lot in common then (or thought they had) and she was baffled by this stranger. The mysteries of one's own past ideas and choices can be greater than the strangeness of other people's choices and opinions. You expect to feel more sympathy and

understanding with your own past self than is sometimes possible. He didn't ask anything at all about her
work, and she was grateful for that. She asked him about
the restaurant with genuine interest, because Kevin and
his job were so closely interrelated that you had to know
about one to know about the other. She was glad when
he said that it was going well; the opposite would have
been worrying. It was a long time since she'd met
someone whose whole sense of self was so closely
bound up in their career, their possessions, their
position in society: without them, she felt, he would be
utterly adrift. They were sitting drinking tea, waiting for
Nuala to come back from Anna's house. 'What are you
thinking, Claire?' he suddenly said. It was the most
intimate question he asked her that day. To answer
honestly she would have had to tell him, 'I just don't
know how I ever thought I loved you.' So of course, she
told him a lie instead.

What colour is happiness? Some people think it's
yellow, but it's really pale blue. Depression: grey, not
black, unless it's really severe, in which case it's red.

He thought she was a failure. Nothing in particular
had to be said for Claire to know that. There were several
possible directions one could take upon leaving art
college. A few people became successful painters, or
went into related careers as photographers, designers or
suchlike. Some became teachers. Others, like Kevin,
accepted that they would make good only by forgetting
about art and moving into an entirely different area:
business or computing or whatever would bring pros-
perity. And then there were people like Claire who
continued working for years at an art which brought

them neither fame nor money, living in spartan rented rooms, always strapped for cash, their creative energy and intellectual curiosity as intense as ever. To Kevin it was pure folly. To Claire, it was life, and a good life.

She knew that when Nuala left Donegal, it was unlikely that they would see each other again, in spite of Nuala having spoken about Claire coming to stay with them in Dublin. Nuala and Kevin having more money than Claire did make a difference, but it was just one strand in a complex web of social pressure and conformity which drew some people together and kept others apart. Like attracted like, the married gravitating to the married, those with children unconsciously seeking out their peers, everyone looking for the like-minded who would bolster them up and confirm their values, beliefs, fears and prejudices. Markus once said to her, 'Take your yearly salary, and then dismiss the possibility of ever getting close to anyone who earns half as much as you, or twice as much as you.' At the time, she had thought he was being cynical, but he had insisted he was right. 'Never underestimate the force of social pressure. That's what makes society run.' No, she wouldn't see them again. This was a period they would want to forget as soon as it had ended, and eliminating Claire from their lives would help them to that end.

She crossed to the window. Too much was made of the sun. The weak northern light had its own beauty; she liked its failure to dominate. She had spent sufficient time on the Continent to know the essence of the south, and the power of the sun, to know that the sun brings death as well as life. She remembered white towns full of hard shadows, and preferred the complexity of the soft light she found in Ireland. It allowed the land, the sky, the ocean to each have their own place. She would never live far from the sea again, its vastness a comfort, its anonymous ancient waves crashing over the detritus of centuries: broken ships, coins, bones, weapons. She would never have believed that it would be possible to feel so much at home.

13

THEY DROVE BACK from Sligo to Donegal on a magnificent summer evening. It had rained earlier in the day, but now the sun had broken through the heavy clouds, blazing fierce gold on the ocean and the rinsed landscape. Everything was radiant, as though the rain had strengthened the essence of the trees and the stones. The sun threw long shadows on the road ahead of them.

Kevin was glad he had come up to see Nuala, and that they had made the trip to Sligo together. He felt something had been resolved between them over the weekend, although he'd have been hard pressed to say exactly what it was, or how the change had been effected. When Claire told him Nuala had turned up safely following her overnight disappearance, he resolved to confront her: to 'have things out' was how he'd phrased it in his own mind. Wasn't that why he had continued on to Donegal? And wasn't that why they had gone to Sligo together, to have the privacy such a discussion demands? And wasn't it typical that 'having it out' was just what they hadn't done?

Evading the issue had been surprisingly easy. Nuala was in an apparently relaxed and amiable frame of mind, and the moment to open a discussion never presented itself. In retrospect, Kevin was amazed at simply how enjoyable the weekend had been. On the Saturday they'd done nothing more strenuous than look around some antique shops (in one of which they bought a clock in a porcelain case), and eat a couple of exceptionally good meals.

But Kevin had lain awake far into Sunday morning, wondering which it was, cowardice or commonsense, that had allowed them to drift through the day without asking the questions which, in the small hours, formed themselves effortlessly (but painfully) in his mind. 'Do you want to leave me? Why did you go away the other night? Why won't you come back to Dublin with me? Did you love your mother more than you love me?'

He felt sure now that they had done the right thing. What had to be said was best said on the level of the remark Nuala made now as she leaned forward to change the cassette in the car stereo.

'I'm ever so glad we got that clock. I wanted to buy something over this summer, something nice that we'll have twenty years from now.'

'You think you'll want to be reminded?'

'I don't think it'll do any harm,' she said. 'I must show it to Anna, I know she'll love it.'

'Anna?'

'You know, the Dutch woman who lives beside Claire. I told you about her.'

'Oh yes, sorry, I forgot. What's she like, this Anna?'

'She's the loneliest person I've ever met,' Nuala said decisively. 'And the worst thing of all is that she doesn't even know it. She likes to think she's a solitary type, but it just isn't true. Claire, now, Claire's a genuine loner. Anna isn't like that, she needs company.'

'You should be careful of her, then,' Kevin said. 'Lame ducks can do more harm than you'd ever believe.'

'But it isn't like that. I feel sorry for her sometimes, but that isn't why I go to see her. She's good company. You wouldn't believe how much she knows about Irish culture and history. Sometimes it embarrasses me, she knows so much more about it than I do.'

Kevin laughed. 'I wouldn't lose too much sleep over that,' he said.

'But it's true,' Nuala said. 'She knows Donegal so well too, and I ought to know it better, what with Mammy being from there.'

'Is she really?' Kevin asked, with fake amazement. 'Now if you hadn't told me that, I'd never have guessed.'

'Kevin! Don't be so mean!'

'Ah, I'm only teasing you, Nuala, but you know what I'm getting at. It didn't matter a damn to your mother that she was from Donegal. She got out of it as fast as she could, and hated going back, even for short visits.'

'Yes, but it's part of my background, whether I like it or not, so maybe it would be good for me to get to know it,' Nuala persisted. Kevin sighed, and this time he wearily agreed with her. He suggested that she make some trips around the county during the remainder of her time there. 'Ask Anna to go with you.' Nuala brightened at this idea, and said she would do that.

'But what about you, Kevin,' she went on. 'Wouldn't you like to get to know Ireland better?'

'No I wouldn't,' he said firmly. 'I know it well enough as it is.'

'But you haven't been back to Tipperary since your granny died, have you?'

By now, Kevin was exasperated. 'Look, Nuala, just be careful. Don't get some false idea stuck in your head about what Ireland is; don't get hung up on some sort of tourist board version of the place. This,' he gestured at the fuschia hedges on either side of the road, 'is Ireland, but so is Dublin. I'm not going to whip myself into some false fervour for the west, and pretend it's somehow more "real" or more wonderful than where we live, and I'd advise you not to do it either.'

There was a pause in the conversation, and he was afraid that he had said too much and soured the atmosphere. 'While you've been away,' he said, 'I've been thinking about holidays. Maybe we'll go somewhere nice in September when you're back home: Paris, Venice even. What do you say?'

'I'd much rather we rented a horse-drawn caravan and did the Ring of Kerry.'

He looked over at her in amazement, and she stared back for a moment, then started to laugh.

'I wish you could see your own face, Kevin, it's a study.'

'I sometimes wonder what I'm ever going to do with you,' Kevin said, but he was laughing too.

They listened to the music as they drove on through the langorous dusk, and Kevin found himself remembering a conversation he'd had with Nuala's doctor around the time she decided to go to Donegal for the summer. They'd been talking about her, and Kevin was surprised when the doctor abruptly asked him, 'Have you ever had a crisis in your life?'

'I'm not sure. What do you mean by "crisis"?'

The doctor laughed. 'Then it's clear that you haven't. I mean losing everything. Oh, not material things, but perhaps everything else: all your self-confidence gone, all your faith in everything you ever believed, everything you felt sure you could count on. Nothing makes sense any more, and you can't understand why.'

Kevin thought about it. No, nothing like that had ever happened to him, and he found it hard to imagine what it must be like.

'What causes it?'

Again the doctor laughed, but this time more gently. 'Life, Kevin, that's what causes it. Past a certain point people begin to take stock of their lives, and sometimes they don't feel good about what they've done. When you're young, you really do think you're immortal. Then one day you realize that it's not true, you aren't going to live for ever. You're born alone and you die alone and everything that comes in between can be pretty lonely too.'

'To tell you the truth, Doctor, I think what you're saying sounds completely banal.'

'But it is!' cried the doctor. 'That's what makes it so hard to bear. The idea of being a martyr, of noble suffering, has a certain dignified appeal to it, but this . . . ! Oh yes, you're right, Kevin: what could be more banal than realizing that you're a human being like any other, and that this is the central tragedy of your life?'

Nuala was humming along with the music now, tapping out the rhythm with her fingertips.

'For how long have you been married now, Kevin?'

'Ten years.'

'My wife and I have been together for twenty years. It's a good thing, marriage. It's different every year, I'm sure you've found that too. Sometimes people come into the surgery and I wish I could write on the prescription pad "Marriage", because it's clear that that's exactly what they need.' He paused a moment. 'Mind you, I must admit I also see some patients for whom I'd like to prescribe a speedy divorce. Still,' he said briskly, 'that's not the case here. Nuala'll be fine, it'll just take time, and perhaps quite a long time too. Look after her, Kevin. She'll be a support to you, I know, when your turn comes.'

'My turn?'

The doctor shook his head and laughed again. 'It doesn't matter. Goodbye, Kevin, and good luck! I'll talk to you again soon.'

'Perhaps New Year would be better,' Nuala said suddenly, and Kevin looked at her blankly. 'To go away,' she said. 'To go to Venice or somewhere.'

'Oh yes, sure, whatever you think.'

Nuala smiled and shook her head.

'What is it?'

'Nothing. Nothing at all.'

The cassette came to an end, and they switched on the radio. They listened to the news first, and then as night fell they listened to the weather forecast, then the shipping forecast. After that there was music again, and they listened to that too, let it wash over them in the blackness as they drove on through the night, until they arrived at last at Claire's house.

14

ANNA WAS DELIGHTED when Nuala suggested that they visit the surrounding area together, and immediately took out her maps and guide books. 'I love this place so much,' she said, 'and it will give me great pleasure to share it with someone else.' They planned a trip for the end of that week to visit a dolmen and a ring of standing stones about an hour's drive away.

But standing in the middle of the stone circle that Friday afternoon, Nuala wondered why she was so disappointed. Was it the old pattern Kevin had pointed out in her so often: expecting too much from things so that disappointment inevitably followed? Perhaps. She knew that was a fault of hers, and a hard habit to break. But this time she wasn't even clear what she had expected from this excursion. Anna too, she thought, was responsible to some degree for Nuala's failure to enjoy the day, for she was in a foul temper. Nuala had never before seen her so tense and irritable. They had gone first to the dolmen. Nuala stood looking blankly at it, as if staring at the stone formation would force it to yield up its secret. 'How old did you say this was?' she asked, and was taken aback when Anna snapped, 'I've already told you at least four times. Why don't you listen? Do you want to tell me to tell you four more?'

Nuala turned her stare from the dolmen to her companion, but said nothing. Anna looked away. 'I'm sorry,' she said. 'I feel wretched. I just couldn't get to sleep at all last night, but there's no reason for me to be taking it out on you.'

'That's all right,' Nuala said. 'I know how you feel, I'm like a bear if I miss a night's sleep. It can't be helped.' She turned back to the strange stone formation, the flat slab on top perched in what seemed to be a precarious position on the lower stones. It looked like you could push the whole construction to the ground with one hand, which was absurd when you considered how solid a thing it actually was. The dolmen had been there for – how many thousands of years? She genuinely couldn't remember, and she didn't dare ask Anna again.

Claire had been surprisingly enthusiastic when Nuala told her where they were going. 'You should have a great day, those are marvellous things to see,' she said. She'd gone on to talk about the spirit of the places, how powerful it was, and the beauty of the stones, their colour and texture. But Nuala felt nothing either at the dolmen or the standing stone circle, nothing but wet and cold and disappointed. The stones were too abstract. The ruins of a church or a weathered statue would perhaps have meant something to her. Some form, some image was necessary for her to connect imaginatively with the distant past. She tried to imagine the ancient people who had placed these stones here, but the stones themselves prevented her from doing so. 'I can't get back to the . . . the simplicity of it,' she said to Anna.

'But what makes you so sure they were simple?' came the immediate response. 'There was probably a complexity there, a sophistication of mind that we can only begin to imagine.'

Anna was beginning to develop an Irish accent, Nuala noted with mild irritation. Her own culture must have been pretty bland if she was able to slough it off like that and effortlessly absorb another. Nuala felt she ought to like the landscape around her. She ought to know more about it and find it as fascinating as Anna did, but she had to admit that it just wasn't the case. The Donegal landscape bored Nuala, just as it had bored her mother, and suddenly she realized how foolish it was to try to connect with her in this way. She closed her eyes and tried to summon up a picture of her mother. She saw her sitting under the hood of a drier at the hairdressers. She could picture her standing in Buckleys debating on equal terms with the butcher about the number of dinners you could reasonably expect to get from the leg of lamb on the slab before them, and she could see her enjoying a gin and tonic before Sunday lunch. Try as she might, though, she couldn't see her standing in a damp field in Donegal getting any sort of interest from looking at a few old lumps of stone.

Anna pulled a silver hip flask from her pocket, drank from it, then silently offered it to Nuala. The brandy scorched down her throat, making her even more aware of how much the damp cold had seeped into her. They went back to the car and ate the sandwiches and cake they had brought with them. Anna drank more of the

brandy. 'I need this,' she said. 'I really need this today.'
Nuala offered to drive afterwards, and Anna, thanking
her, willingly handed over the keys.

They had only gone a few miles when they came to a
small church. Anna insisted that they stop to visit it.
Nuala wasn't so keen. 'Maybe it won't be open,' she
said.

'Of course it will,' said Anna. 'Churches in the country
in Ireland are always open, that's one of the things I like
about them.' As they walked from the car, Anna started
to explain why Catholic churches in Ireland were often
so far from centres of population, when Nuala interrupted her, and said she already knew about that. Did
the woman think she was completely ignorant of her
own country and religion?

The church was a low, solid building without a spire.
As Anna had predicted, it was unlocked. It was also
empty, and unremarkable. Nuala had seen many
churches like this in the past, and it was evidently
familiar territory for Anna, too. Like all old churches, it
reminded Nuala of her childhood. The altar rails had
been taken away and the altar itself had been moved out
from the wall as a token gesture to the reforms of Vatican
Two, but otherwise nothing had changed: the plaster
statues, the simple posies of wallflowers, the candles,
the smell of wax and incense, the powerful silence.

Anna settled herself comfortably in a pew at the back
of the church, and gestured to Nuala to come and sit
beside her.

'Isn't it nice the way they keep the churches unlocked
here, so that anyone can go into them,' Anna said
companionably, in her normal tone of voice. This

unnerved Nuala, who had been brought up to whisper in church, and still felt uncomfortable to do otherwise, or even to hear anyone else speak aloud. But she didn't dare tell Anna to speak lower, so she listened miserably as her friend continued. 'On the Continent, apart from cathedrals in the cities that are open for the tourists, they keep all the churches locked. If God existed, he would die of loneliness.' She laughed, and Nuala felt even more uncomfortable. 'It has to be like that, of course, or people would go in and steal things, or desecrate the place.

'A couple went into a church a few years ago, I forget where, I think it was in Spain, and had sex on a side altar. Just imagine. They were caught, of course, and severely punished. I suppose the courts thought that if they let them off lightly it would have become a craze amongst the young. They'd all have been doing it, and then other people would have got upset.'

Nuala didn't say anything. 'What do you believe in?' Anna asked her a few moments later. Nuala's reply, when it came, was mumbled so low that Anna asked her to repeat it.

'I said, I don't know.'

'Of course you don't, how can anyone know?' said Anna. 'Then again, there are people who think that they know. Take Rita, for instance. Rita fascinates me. She has blind faith. I find that quite extraordinary. I can't begin to understand it, and I told her so too. I said her religion was a mystery to me. She said it was a mystery to her. She went to Lourdes last summer. I wanted to ask her, "Can you honestly tell me that you believe all this . . . this nonsense?" Yes, I wanted to ask her, but I didn't dare. I knew she would be offended, and I didn't want that because I like Rita. I genuinely like and respect her. She's a good woman.'

No, Nuala didn't know what she believed any longer, and she rarely gave it any thought. She hardly ever went to Mass and when she did, she felt vaguely uneasy, as though there were something false about her being there. But then again, she also felt guilty not going. 'We ought to go to Mass more often,' she said to Kevin one Sunday morning over the usual late breakfast and pile of newspapers.

'Less of the "we", please,' he'd replied. 'Don't try to offload your Catholic guilt on to me. Go to Mass if you feel like it, I won't stop you.'

'It's not that I want to, I just feel I ought to,' she'd said. Kevin had put down his paper. 'Nuala, if I had a fiver for every time I'd heard you say you ought to do something or other, I could close the restaurant tomorrow and retire to the south of France. If you really ought to be doing these things you talk about, then go and do them. Otherwise put them out of your mind and stop tormenting yourself. And me.'

It was all very well for Kevin to say that. About a month after her mother died, Nuala was coming out of the Powerscourt Centre when she noticed the Carmelite church in the street beside it. She had gone into it to say a prayer for her mother, because she wanted to, but also because she felt that she should do so. She thought about her mother constantly, but she never prayed for her. Perhaps by now she had forgotten how to pray, it was such a long time since she had tried, or had given it any serious attention. When she went into the church and knelt down, she was disconcerted to find how difficult it was for her to focus her mind, and dismiss all the stray thoughts that crowded in, as persistent as they were trivial. She felt self-conscious kneeling there with her eyes squeezed shut, and after a few moments she gave up. She sat down, and just thought about her mother. She didn't know what she believed about what had happened to her. The idea that she had been completely annihilated was as impossible for Nuala to believe as the thought of her being in some cotton-wool-clouded heaven. The only thing she knew for sure was that she missed her more than she would have ever thought possible.

'I like these country churches,' Anna said, glancing around her. 'I like the sentimentality, the kitsch. There's a simplicity of thought behind them that you don't see anywhere else. Yes, I like them a lot, but if I am to be honest, I must say that I also despise them a little bit too.'

'Why?'

'Because they do enormous harm to people. Catholicism can break people's spirits like nothing else. People cannot abide the idea of purity, you know. Complete purity, physical and mental, is impossible for any human being, and for most, it is so far above them that it angers them. It is showing people something, telling them that this is the highest good and that they ought to strive for it, but of course it's impossible, they will never manage it. And so they grow angry and bitter, as is only to be expected. It's particularly dangerous for women, because it's aimed more at them, to keep them in their place, and then women have such scrupulous minds, I always think. The image the church presents of women is bad because it is incomplete. Do you know anything about the ancient religions, Nuala? No? They are good, they are very wise,' said Anna, who was choosing her words carefully. 'These religions are mentally sound, not like Christianity which is fundamentally neurotic, and so the end is neurosis. The ancient religions are more complete, their gods and goddesses are more psychologically true, more complex, more in the image of humanity than is the case with Christianity. And yet you know, there is something very strange in this: that Ireland isn't a Christian country at all. What I like about Ireland is that just below this crust of Catholicism it is pure paganism, not like where I come from, where it is Protestantism crusting over nihilism. And so you have the priests telling the women to be like Mary and some of them are trying, some of them are pretending, and some of them just don't give a damn, because they are in touch with their own reality, they understand their own selves in a very deep, real way. They are free.' She pointed up at the statue.

'Some people think that the worst thing about Catholicism is that it sees women only in terms of their reproductive capacity, sees them only as mothers. But that is only part of it. The real problem is that they portray mothers as being only good, as being only like Mary: pure and long-suffering and selfless. But deep down, every woman knows that it's not the whole story. Mothers have their dark side too.' Her voice was full of derision. 'Why, everyone knows that, even little children reading their fairy stories, where the cruel mother is a stepmother to make it a little more bearable for them. Everybody knows it, everybody who's had a mother or been one, and yet this lie is maintained, no one wants to talk about it out loud. Mothers can be good and bad. That's why I don't like this religion.' She looked across at Nuala, but Nuala wasn't shocked, as Anna had thought she would be. She was looking hard at her, trying to work out what was at the back of all this. For a moment, she thought Nuala was going to ask her what was wrong, but she evidently thought better of it. Nuala looked grave and thoughtful, but she said nothing.

Anna wished she were weaker, wished that she would break down and tell her friend what was troubling her. It wasn't that she thought Nuala could help, she just wanted to talk to another person about it. Others confided in her, why couldn't she do the same? No, she was too ashamed. Too proud. But then, wasn't that what Lili had always said about her, that she was too proud?

When they were outside the church again, Nuala took another hard look at Anna. She could well believe that she had missed a night's sleep. She looked haggard and older than Nuala had seen her looking before, older than she probably was. 'Are you sure you feel all right?' she asked tentatively. 'Is anything troubling you?'

At first Anna did not reply, then she said, 'What difference has it made to you, having your baby? If your mother had still been alive, do you think it would have brought you closer?'

Nuala's reply to this was to turn her back on the other woman. 'Why do you want to hurt me?' she said eventually.

How must it be to be vulnerable like this? Anna thought. Why was she cursed with what seemed like strength, but which was really such a handicap, such a stupid thing. She wanted to tell Nuala why she was upset, but she couldn't do it. She just couldn't make herself say the necessary words.

'I'm sorry,' she said at last. 'I didn't mean to hurt you, although I can see that I have. Please forgive me.' Nuala turned to her, and put her arms round her. She hugged the older woman tightly, and was kind enough to pretend not to see the tears that this brought to her eyes.

15

EVELIEN, THE WOMAN with whom Anna had first visited Ireland, was her oldest and best friend. They had been to school together, and during the winter, when Anna was back in Holland, they saw each other frequently. Neither woman was a good correspondent: in the course of the summer a postcard was usually as much communication as there would be between them. The day before Anna went to the stone circle with Nuala, however, she had a letter from Evelien.

As she picked up the envelope in the hall, Anna's pleasure when she recognized the handwriting quickly changed to unease. A letter from her friend was such an unusual event that Anna felt sure it must contain bad news. She ripped the envelope open and scanned the letter impatiently. It was a long, rambling missive, but Anna quickly got to the hard, bald fact around which it was constructed. Then she went to the sitting-room cupboard, poured a shot of whiskey and knocked it straight back. She waited a few moments and then repeated this with a larger measure of whiskey. It was half past nine in the morning. She sat still and quiet for some time. Then she picked up the letter again, and this time she read it slowly and carefully, paying attention to every word.

Evelien had written to tell Anna that Lili had had a baby. She was clearly embarrassed to be doing so, and therefore the letter was full of generalities, this main piece of news treated in an almost throwaway fashion. Evelien was tactful enough to pretend that of course Anna knew all about this, but kind enough to include such details as anyone in Anna's position would want to know. The baby was a girl, now aged about four months. Evelien had been sitting in a café when Lili came in with another woman, and sat at a nearby table. She didn't notice Evelien, and Evelien confessed that she hadn't drawn attention to herself. On the contrary: she'd hidden behind a newspaper and peeped around it at the young woman, catching the odd fragment of her conversation. Because of the rift between Lili and Anna, Evelien would have felt hypocritical approaching Lili. In any case, she would probably have been snubbed. Evelien thought Lili was being unfair to her mother and she'd once gone so far as to tell her so, and of course it had ended in a quarrel. But with quiet insistence, Evelien left Anna in no doubt about the circumstances. From things she'd overheard, it was absolutely clear that the baby was Lili's own, not a friend's child she was looking after. She also remarked that it was a long time since she'd seen anyone looking so contented and happy.

Anna folded up the letter, and carefully put it back into the envelope. She went to the kitchen and made a pot of strong coffee.

Well, she'd thought this might happen. Tell the truth, hadn't she even hoped it might happen? But not like this. No, never like this. If Lili became a mother, Anna

131

had always thought, it would ease Anna's conscience, by proving that she hadn't turned her daughter off the idea of families completely. Did she feel that relief now? Yes, to some extent. But she'd also hoped that it would bring a change of heart, that when Lili was a mother herself she would understand why Anna had behaved as she did, and then they would be reconciled. But Lili hadn't bothered to let Anna know that she was pregnant. She'd had the baby and told her mother nothing, and this cut Anna to the heart. She thought of Evelien, who knew how much Anna wanted to be on better terms with her daughter. Once, Anna had even suggested to Evelien, 'I could pretend to be sick, couldn't I? I mean if I were really sick she would have to know, and she might see things differently then.'

'But you aren't ill,' Evelien had said sharply. 'And if you lied to her about that, just as a way of getting close to her again, she would never forgive you when she found out.' Evelien was the only person who knew the lengths to which Anna was prepared to go in this matter. That was why she had written, and why she had been so tactful. She alone knew how deeply hurt Anna would be. Hurt and ashamed.

She brooded on this news for the rest of the day, and that night she couldn't sleep. The trip with Nuala had been arranged for the following morning, and they set out as planned, but it all went badly. Nuala appeared bored by the places they visited, and this annoyed Anna, who felt tense and short tempered. She knew she tended to take things out on Nuala sometimes because she reminded her of Lili. She was also aware of how unfair this was, but today she didn't care, because it was foolish to expect fairness in life. Was it fair that her husband had left her and wrecked their marriage? That she could become a grandmother without her daughter bothering to tell her about it? That Nuala's mother had died before Nuala's baby had been born? Where was the fairness in any of that? But she pushed Nuala too far that day, and regretted it afterwards when it was too late, and Nuala was clearly upset.

At the end of that week Claire also received a letter, which she opened at breakfast. 'It's from Mammy,' she said to Nuala, laughing.

'What's the joke?'

Claire passed to Nuala a photograph which her mother had enclosed with the letter, and Nuala began to laugh too.

'Look at us! What are we like? I've never seen this photo before, have you?'

'Yes, but I'd forgotten all about it. I can even remember the day it was taken. It was Granny's seventieth birthday, and there was a little family party. You came up from Dublin with your parents and stayed with us, do you remember?'

'I can barely remember that, although I know we did it. We were very small then. How old, four? Five?'

'About that. It was summer, and we were both going to start school in the autumn, and you already knew all the alphabet and could count much higher than I could.' Nuala passed the photograph back to her, and Claire studied it. Her memories of the visit were much more vivid and complete than she was prepared to tell Nuala, for she didn't remember her cousin in a particularly flattering light. She'd looked forward to seeing her relatives from Dublin, and how disappointed she'd been. Her parents wanted her to play with Nuala, but Nuala was aloof, and wanted only to stay with her mother the whole time. Auntie Kate had indulged her in this, hugging Nuala and saying of course she didn't have to go outside if she didn't want to. Even as a child Claire could see how much this annoyed her own mother, who hated children sitting listening in to adult conversation.

'I'll take you out and show you the farmyard,' Claire had offered. 'I'll show you the pigs.'

Nuala shook her head, and buried her face in her mother's side.

'See the pigs, indeed,' said Auntie Kate, as though this were the most ridiculous suggestion in the world. Nuala preferred to show off her superior learning. Twenty-five,' she said slowly. 'Twenty-six. Twenty-seven.'

Claire didn't like Auntie Kate. She pretended to be nice to you, but Claire knew it was all put on. 'You don't like her either, do you Mammy?' she'd said, and was surprised when her mother said, 'Why, what gave you that idea? I like Auntie Kate very much, don't ever let me hear you say things like that again.' She'd overheard her father saying to her mother on the way home from Granny's party, 'That Nuala one's as old-fashioned as a field,' and, remembering this over thirty years later, Claire smiled as she glanced up from the photograph to Nuala, innocently buttering toast on the other side of the table.

The Christmas after the party Auntie Kate had sent Claire a pound note, and for the first time ever Claire didn't have that warm contented feeling you usually got when someone gave you money. She'd put the pound in her purse, but looking at it had made her feel uneasy. It wasn't like when Granny gave you a half crown when it was as good just to have it as to spend it. She didn't realize that she was experiencing for the first time the difference between a thing itself and its emotional connection. She just knew she wanted to spend the money on sweets that she could eat and then forget. She didn't want to use the money to buy something lasting, that would sit around reminding her unpleasantly of Auntie Kate every time she looked at it.

Claire would have been surprised to realize just how much Nuala also remembered of that visit: far more than she was prepared to admit. She could even recall the journey up to Donegal, and how her mother had kept pulling at her fingers to make the bones crack, until Nuala's father asked her to stop, and she did, for a while but then started it again. They'd stopped somewhere to have a meal in a hotel, and Nuala and her mother had gone off to the toilet together. 'Stand by that basin and wait for me,' her mother commanded, before darting into a cubicle. Nuala heard the bolt click, then the unmistakable sound of someone being sick. Her mother came out, her eyes unusually bright. 'Don't tell Daddy, Nuala. He'd only be cross with me.' Nuala nodded, and felt her own tummy tighten. She didn't know what all this was about, but she knew she didn't like it.

She didn't like the farm either when she got there. It wasn't how she had imagined it would be from picture books about farms. There was a strange, sourish smell in the dark kitchen. They'd sat down on a sofa, and she'd clung to her mother. She could see Auntie Pat didn't like her much, which was a shock: no one had ever not liked

135

Nuala before in her life. She clung more tightly to her mother in hurt and defiance, refusing to be wooed out to the farmyard to see the animals. They'd wanted her to play with Claire until her mother defended her, and said Nuala didn't have to do anything she didn't want to do.

On the journey back to Dublin they stopped off again in the same hotel. This time Nuala stood by the basin and watched her mother putting on some vivid lipstick. She smiled indulgently when she noticed her daughter's fixed gaze, and, bending down, put some lipstick on her too. Nothing held a greater fascination for Nuala than her mother's make-up bag, and her mother only allowed her access to it when she was in an exceptionally good mood. She tried to imagine being grown up and having a bag like that of her own, but it was beyond her. 'Here, look.' Her mother fished out a little pot of rouge and offered it to Nuala. 'Yes, you can keep it. It's yours now. When we get back to Dublin I'll have a look and see what else I have that you might like. We'll do something nice tomorrow, too, something special. I know! We'll go to the zoo! Just the two of us, would you like that?'

Nuala gazed up at her. She would never in all her life love anyone as she loved her mother in that moment.

16

FOR ABOUT AN HOUR NOW, Claire had been sitting on a hard kitchen chair in her studio, smoking cigarettes and looking at the paintings she had done over the course of the summer. First she arranged them all around the studio in careful sequence, and then simply sat looking at them. She stared at each one in turn, and then considered it first in relation to the pictures on either side of it, and then to the whole cycle of paintings. Occasionally she would stand up and rearrange the sequence slightly, then sit down again to consider the effect of this change. Once she got up and removed a canvas completely from the arrangement, propping it behind her chair, with the image facing the wall.

The longer she looked at the paintings, the more uncertain she became about their merits and failings. It was not just possible but necessary to look at them in different ways. At first, she tried to evaluate them in terms of their being her own work. How did they compare with paintings she had done in the past? Did they fulfil the intentions she had had when she embarked on the project? If not, did that matter? Was she satisfied with the work?

Of course not. She was never satisfied. Only dissatisfaction could drive her on, keep her painting in the hope that the next time would be better, while knowing always that it would never be good enough.

The paintings were based on a series of anatomical drawings she had made two years earlier. For a long time her work had been heavily emotional, and the drawings, red chalk on paper, had been an attempt to change direction. Before assessing the pictures today, she had looked again at the slides of the drawings, remembering how fascinated she had become by pure form, while still knowing that it wasn't enough. She'd looked at the spine then as though it weren't a spine, just an extraordinarily complex and beautiful structure. She'd drawn fans of muscle and the joints of fingers as though they had nothing at all to do with the human body. Then one day, while out walking, she came across a magnificent escarpment of fissured rock. Slabs of stone had fallen cleanly away, leaving a series of flat planes. She'd wanted to paint it immediately, but without reference to the surrounding landscape or the sky. No, just the rocks themselves, their colour and texture and form. Then she'd laid her hand upon the stone, her warm, living hand upon the cold inanimate stone, and suddenly knew the drawings were a blind alley.

She'd changed medium, hoping that by going back to painting again she would find it easier to combine form and feeling in the way she desired. Now she painted bones and muscles as though they were not just beautiful abstractions, but also parts of a strong and vulnerable body. Well, that was what she had tried to do, and she still wasn't at all sure that she had succeeded.

She got up abruptly from the chair and walked over to

the window, feeling that she would be sick if she looked at the paintings for one more minute. Alice had said to her once, 'There are days when what I like most about painting is that you're making something, you're left with something solid at the end of it, and there are other days when I hate it, for that very reason.' She'd been sitting on the floor of her own studio when she said this, surrounded by paintings which she was preparing to put in store. 'You work and you work and then you're left with all these *things* and you don't know what to do with them. It must be great to be a musician creating nothing more tangible than sound.'

'And do you really think you'd prefer that?'

Alice had laughed at that. 'Of course not. I'm only griping because these pictures will take up the last of my storage space, and after that I just don't know where the hell I'm going to keep my work. I'm also fed up trying to scrape together the money I need to buy paints and canvas, so I can see the appeal of an art form that requires minimal space and materials. But what I love about it too is just that: the energy of things. I like the paradox of it. Strength and frailty, don't you see? People confuse immortality with the indestructible, but it's not the same thing at all. Take, say, Vermeer's *Portrait Of a Young Woman in a Turban*. What that painting means is beyond words, beyond time. And yet, in purely material terms, it's a layer of paint a couple of millimetres thick on a piece of canvas.'

'What you're saying is that it's more than a sum of its parts?'

'No, what I'm saying is that it's so much more that it's beyond comprehension, it's almost eerie. That's the magic of it, the only magic I could ever believe in. To take things and make something charged with that sort of knowledge and energy. It's worth devoting your life to that.'

Material permanence: as terrible a concept as perfect memory. Claire ran her finger through the dust on the windowsill. Sea glass, shells, a fragment of bark. Petals that had fallen from a vase of roses. She bent over the flowers and breathed in their deep, heavy scent. Two flat pieces of stone that fitted together like a cut fruit, a fossil of a horsetail fern on either side when you split them apart. How many millions of years?

It was raining outside. She rubbed the back of her hand across the misted glass. When she came into the studio on a winter's morning sometimes the windows would be iced on the inside, with thick swirls of frost flowers. She would admire them, then put her mouth close to the glass and melt them with a long hot breath. The wind was blowing hard too. It was often stormy in August, but then sometimes the weather would settle down again in September and be calm and fine for a week or so. But in August you could already sense the start of winter: there was a new edge to the cold.

Nuala would be leaving soon. How different people were from each other, and how separate they seemed doomed to remain! 'Try to see it from my point of view,' she'd said to Claire one day in the course of conversation, and Claire had known, even without attempting it, that she wouldn't be able to do it. Certainly they'd got to know each other better during the time Nuala had been there, and she'd become quite fond of her, but Claire knew they would always be isolated from each other at a fundamental level. Maybe it could only be like that. How much of one's self was it possible to communicate to another person? Probably far less than is generally admitted. Imagine being able to enter into another person's mind, even for just a few moments. It was bound to be a revelation, particularly if it was someone you thought you knew well, and a shock to see how far one's perception of a person could be from how that person actually saw themselves.

'Look at the cut of me!' Claire's mother had said the last time she'd visited her. She'd been sitting by a mirror, combing out her faded hair. 'I'm as grey as a badger. How come I look so old, yet I feel no different to what I was forty years ago? Where's the sense in that?' She'd started to laugh, and added, 'I remember when I was a child, I used to look at my grandmother and marvel at just how old somebody could be; it almost frightened me. And then the other day when I was in town I saw this little girl looking at me and looking at me, and suddenly I realized, "As far as she's concerned, I'm an old lady." And so I did a few calculations, and do you know, I'm older now already than my grandmother was when she died. I could hardly believe it, so I told your daddy, and he said, "Well then, that proves it. You *are* an old lady!"'

Claire understood exactly what her mother meant, but it wasn't the whole story. You *did* change. Life changed you, whether you liked it or not. You saw options that you'd always taken for granted in life close for ever. You suddenly realized that you were going to die someday. 'Painting's a bit like life,' she'd said to Nuala the previous evening, when their conversation had edged towards this same subject. 'There's no point in just sitting there thinking about it. You have to get the paint on to the canvas. You may not like what you end up with; it may fall short of what you had thought or hoped it would be – in fact, it usually does. But at least there's something there; at least it's real.'

'When I was a child,' Nuala had said, 'I used to look forward to being grown up. I was always trying to imagine how it would be. And sometimes now I look at my life and say to myself, "Well, now you know." But it still doesn't fit, it doesn't add up. Not,' she added quickly, 'that I don't like my life. No, not that. I'm a very lucky person; it's a good life. No, it's not that I don't like it, it's . . . it's that . . .' Her voice trailed away.

'It's that you don't understand it,' Claire said.

'Something like that,' Nuala mumbled, looking at her hands. Claire nodded.

'And yes, you're right,' she added. 'You are lucky. We all are.'

'All?'

'You, me, Kevin: we're lucky. Our lives are good. Maybe not always what we would want, but good, for all that.'

'The door of the studio, which had been slightly ajar, suddenly banged shut with a force that made Claire jump up from the windowsill in fright. She listened, and then she could hear Nuala moving about in the kitchen. She must have just come into the house, and in opening the front door created a draught that made the studio door slam. Claire didn't like unexplained movements and noises in the house. She'd have been ashamed to admit to anyone how nervous she was, even how superstitious . . . was it superstition? Perhaps she should tell someone about what had happened all those years ago, but she'd never been able to bring herself to do so.

On the first anniversary of Alice's death, Claire had made a small memorial to her. Because she had been abroad when Alice died and had missed her funeral, she felt she hadn't had a chance to say goodbye to her properly. She therefore decided to make something for Alice, just for that day. On a table in a corner of the studio, she'd set up what amounted to a secular altar. The painting Alice had given her had formed the centrepiece. She put a white candle on the table, and vases full of cut flowers.

She worked as usual that day, and would glance up at the table in the corner now and again. Years had passed, but it still made Claire shiver to think about what had happened.

Late in the forenoon, the phone had rung. She went into the next room and picked up the receiver, but there was silence at the other end. As she hung up, she heard a crash from the studio.

Something had destroyed the memorial. The painting was still on the table, but the floor was a mess of flowers, water, broken glass, melted wax from the extinguished candle. She knew at once that however much she wanted to, she would never be able to explain this away. No draughts: the studio door was wedged open, every other door and window firmly shut. No one else was in the house; there was no cat to blame. The wreckage was a good six feet away from the table. The flowers and candle had not simply fallen over, they had been swept violently to the floor.

She'd been so frightened and upset that it was hours before she could even bring herself to clear away the mess. There was fear, too, in her reluctance to tell anyone. She didn't want to disturb things even more. It would vulgarize it to tell people. It would become a story friends would tell friends, 'I know someone and the strangest thing happened to her.' It would be exaggerated, embroidered, cheapened. But nothing would explain it. Nothing could.

In succeeding years, she had ignored Alice's anniversary, tried not even to think about her on that day. Nothing of the kind had ever happened again, but sudden noises startled Claire, even when there was a simple explanation. She turned again to the sequence of paintings. The impact they made when she looked at them this time pleased her more than before, pleased her more than she would have expected.

17

'MAYBE YOU WON'T LIKE ME for this,' Nuala said. 'Maybe you'll never forgive me, but we probably won't ever see each other again, so I'm going to risk it.' Anna smiled and put her head to one side. 'You already know what I'm going to ask you.'

'Do I?' said Anna.

'Yes, you do. But you're pretending you don't, to make it as difficult as possible for me.'

It was the evening before Nuala's departure, and she had come to say goodbye to Anna. They had been sitting by the fire for over two hours now, and darkness was falling. Anna did not get up to draw the curtains and switch on the lights. On the contrary: it was as though by tacit agreement that they waited for the dark, talking only of inconsequential things while they could still see each other clearly. The only light in the room came from the flames in the hearth.

'Don't think badly of me, Nuala. Yes, I know exactly what you're going to ask me.'

'And you don't mind?'

'Let me just make this condition: that I can ask you exactly the same question, which is this: What's wrong?'

Now it was Nuala's turn to smile. 'You see, you did know.'

'So answer me. I'm asking you first. What's wrong?'

Nuala was silent, but Anna didn't persist. She allowed her the time she knew she needed. The silence stretched out. The clock ticked. The fire collapsed in on itself with a hushed sound, and then the flames began to burn more brightly than before, throwing shadows across the room. There was rain falling against the window, and a wind rising. Nuala didn't want to answer because she didn't want to break the peace of the moment, or lose the kindness of Anna's waiting silence. After a long time she spoke.

'I'm unhappy because I don't know how to live.'

Anna did not reply. It was so dark now that Nuala could not see the expression on the other woman's face at all, just the outline of her where she sat. Nuala felt warm and calm. She listened again to the fire, the rain, the clock, and only gradually did she notice another sound. Anna was crying.

'Oh Nuala,' she said eventually. 'How to live: do you really think that any of us know that?'

Anna insisted on keeping her side of the agreement, even though Nuala kept saying that it didn't matter, afraid that Anna would become even more upset.

'I'm going to tell you,' Anna said. 'I promised I would and I try to always keep my word. I probably should have talked to you like this a long time ago.'

'Well then,' said Nuala, 'when you're ready.'

Slowly and very quietly Anna told Nuala about how her marriage had broken up, and how Lili blamed her for it. She told her that she'd heard over the summer that

Lili had had a baby. She hadn't even told Anna she was pregnant, and she couldn't bear it that her own daughter was so cold to her – that she hated her so much.

Nuala said nothing while Anna spoke, and listened patiently to the end.

'Well,' she said eventually, 'you're right about one thing at least: you should have talked about this before now, to me, or to somebody. You shouldn't have kept it bottled up all these years. Because you've got it all completely wrong, don't you see?'

'What do you mean?'

'Lili doesn't blame you. I'd bet my life on that.'

'But she does, I know. She's told me so.'

'And you deny it every time. The one thing you insist on is that it's not *your* fault. So she knows you don't blame yourself. Then who does she think you do hold responsible?'

'My husband, of course.'

'No Anna,' Nuala said. 'Not your husband. Lili thinks you blame her.'

'Lili? But it's not possible, it's ridiculous. You don't understand. She was a child of ten when it happened.'

'Precisely.' Nuala paused to let this sink in.

'But she's never said this to me, never in all these years.'

'Well, she wouldn't, would she? Because if she did, you'd have denied it, just as you've denied it to me right now. So she's been waiting for you to make the first move and you never did. You've only ever defended yourself, and she's given up waiting.'

Anna was still having trouble taking this in. 'Just think about it,' Nuala said. 'You'll see I'm right. Anna, I'm

147

being very blunt with you. Maybe you have left it too late. Maybe she'll never forgive you. But then again, she just might. There's no knowing.'

'So what should I do?' Anna said.

'You're going to have to make the first move,' Nuala said, 'and you're going to have to take it very gently. You could buy something nice for the baby here in Ireland, and then send it to her when you get home, with a card or a letter saying that you want to be on good terms with her. Explain that you see now how she must have felt. Ask her to forgive you.' She could see Anna balk at this, and added quickly. 'I didn't say this would be easy. Remember it's not just a question of swallowing your pride. Don't make any approach to her until you're reasonably convinced that what I'm saying is correct. And don't expect miracles. Maybe she won't want to have anything to do with you. Even if she does, it'll probably take her a long time to thaw out. Just go gently, and give it lots of time.'

'Do you think it'll work?' Anna said timidly.

'I wish I could say yes,' Nuala said. 'But I just don't know. I hope it does. Will you write and tell me?'

'Yes of course,' said Anna. 'And you must write to me too, to tell me how things are.'

Nuala smiled to herself, again grateful for the darkness. She had gone down to the beach that afternoon and thrown her teaspoon into the waves. Maybe it would be washed up on the beach and someone would find it. They'd wonder how a spoon from a hotel in Dublin came to be on a beach in Donegal. They'd never guess.

Nuala was surprisingly decisive about her departure.

She insisted on going back to Dublin as she had arrived, rather than have Kevin travel up to Donegal to collect her. Anna offered to drive Nuala into town to catch the bus, an offer which was accepted.

'Please don't wait to see me off,' she said to Claire. 'Go and start your work as usual, I don't want to hold you back.' Claire went along with this, keen to avoid sitting around with her for twenty minutes or so, with their goodbyes made and nothing else to do but grow tense and awkward with each other. Relieved, she went upstairs to her studio.

Over the course of the summer, Claire had stopped painting the view from the window, and started to draw a still life every morning instead. For the past week now she had been drawing the same apple over and over, trying to catch its essence as quickly and simply as possible. This morning, she deliberately worked slowly, waiting to hear Nuala leave the house. She knew she wouldn't be able to settle to her real work today until she was alone, even though she hadn't been bothered by Nuala's presence all summer. She drew a line with a soft pencil, then smudged it with her finger, and put her eye close to the sketch book. The paper was soft and fuzzy, like the skin of a peach; the pencil mark was pearly.

She wouldn't see Nuala any more often than she had done in the past, but through her family she would always know how she was, and what she was doing. It struck her as absurd that this should be so, while she would probably never hear of Markus ever again or know where he was, or what he was doing; and yet she still thought about him all the time. She had dreamt about him the night before, and remembered when she woke that what she had dreamt of had once actually happened, but she had forgotten it until now.

They'd travelled a lot during the time they were together, mainly in Germany and France. One hot afternoon, they had sat at a pavement café in Paris, drinking wine. At the gates of a nearby church, an old woman was begging. The passers-by ignored her: no one gave her anything, and most of them looked straight through her, as though her age and her poverty had rendered her invisible. Claire looked at her face: it was hard to imagine that she had ever been young.

Markus didn't notice the woman until Claire pointed her out to him.

'Before God,' she said, 'we are all like that.' She could see that this angered him: she had known it would, but she persisted. 'Don't you see how the people shun her? In her weakness and destitution they recognize something of themselves, and it frightens them. They want to deny it, so they try to pretend that she doesn't even exist.' He stared at her coldly, and she realized then that their life together was over.

'Why do you despise people?' he asked, after a moment's pause.

'I don't, Markus, and you know that I don't.'

'What do you feel, then, when you look at the world? When you look at this?' And he gestured at the street.

She was going to say, 'Pity,' but when she spoke, she said, 'Love.'

She picked up the apple she had been drawing, and examined it as closely as she had examined the texture of the page which bore its image. The fruit had lost its lustre during the days she had kept it in the studio. The skin was puckered and shrunken; and the deep fragrant scent of the apple had diminished to an unpleasantly sweet smell, redolent of decay. What would she draw tomorrow? A loaf. Roses. More fruit.

Sometimes it was easy to forget that life was driven by necessity. The world today conspired to induce such forgetfulness. What was worth knowing in life? The limits, the severe limits of one's understanding and abilities, the power of love and forgiveness; and that life was nothing if not mysterious.

She heard a car drive up to the house. The front door slammed, she heard voices, then the car drove away again and there was silence. Claire put aside the sketch book, and turned her attention to her real work.